She'd conceived Jack's child.

Jennifer sank back in the chair and splayed her hands on her flat stomach.

Jack's baby, her mind whispered. No, it was *her* baby. Her secret. She was not going to tell Jack about this child unless he came to her and asked her to marry him.

She wouldn't trap him into proposing to her, thus sentencing herself to a lifetime of wondering if he truly wished to be by her side.

If Jack went to California per his original plan, he would never, ever know that this child existed.

And the serious discussion she'd scheduled for that evening? Oh, yes, they'd have that talk, but she'd keep a tight rein on her emotions. She'd wait to hear what Jack had to say.

Wait…while she hoped and prayed that he'd ask her to be his wife.…

Dear Reader,

Welcome to a spectacular month of great romances as we continue to celebrate Silhouette's 20th Anniversary all year long!

Beloved bestselling author Nora Roberts returns with *Irish Rebel,* a passionate sequel to her very first book, *Irish Thoroughbred.* Revisit the spirited Grant family as tempers flare, sparks fly and love ignites between the newest generation of Irish rebels!

Also featured this month is Christine Flynn's poignant THAT'S MY BABY! story, *The Baby Quilt,* in which a disillusioned, high-powered attorney finds love and meaning in the arms of an innocent young mother.

Silhouette reader favorite Joan Elliott Pickart delights us with her secret baby story, *To a MacAllister Born,* adding to her heartwarming cross-line miniseries, THE BABY BET. And acclaimed author Ginna Gray delivers the first compelling story in her series, A FAMILY BOND, with *A Man Apart,* in which a wounded loner lawman is healed heart, body and soul by the nurturing touch of a beautiful, compassionate woman.

Rounding off the month are two more exciting ongoing miniseries. From longtime author Susan Mallery, we have a sizzling marriage-of-convenience story, *The Sheik's Secret Bride,* the third book in her DESERT ROGUES series. And Janis Reams Hudson once again shows her flair for Western themes and Native American heroes with *The Price of Honor,* a part of her miniseries, WILDERS OF WYATT COUNTY.

It's a terrific month of page-turning reading from Special Edition. Enjoy!

All the best,

Karen Taylor Richman
Senior Editor

Please address questions and book requests to:
Silhouette Reader Service
U.S.: 3010 Walden Ave., P.O. Box 1325, Buffalo, NY 14269
Canadian: P.O. Box 609, Fort Erie, Ont. L2A 5X3

JOAN ELLIOTT PICKART

TO A MacALLISTER BORN

Silhouette®

SPECIAL EDITION®

Published by Silhouette Books

America's Publisher of Contemporary Romance

For my daughter, Paige,
my very own Tempe, Arizona, fire fighter

I'm a proud mommy, Peep

SILHOUETTE BOOKS

ISBN 0-373-24329-4

TO A MacALLISTER BORN

This edition published by arrangement with Harlequin Books S.A.

® and TM are trademarks of Harlequin Books S.A., used under license.
Trademarks indicated with ® are registered in the United States Patent
and Trademark Office, the Canadian Trade Marks Office and in other
countries.

Visit Silhouette at www.eHarlequin.com

Printed in U.S.A.

Books by Joan Elliott Pickart

Silhouette Special Edition

*Friends, Lovers...and
  Babies!* #1011
The Father of Her Child #1025
†*Texas Dawn* #1100
†*Texas Baby* #1141
‡*Wife Most Wanted* #1160
*The Rancher and the Amnesiac
  Bride* #1204
Δ*The Irresistible Mr.
  Sinclair* #1256
Δ*The Most Eligible M.D.* #1262
*Man...Mercenary...
  Monarch* #1303
To a MacAllister Born #1329

Silhouette Desire

Angels and Elves #961
Apache Dream Bride #999
†*Texas Moon* #1051
†*Texas Glory* #1088
Just My Joe #1202
Δ*Taming Tall, Dark Brandon* #1223

*The Baby Bet
†Family Men
‡Montana Mavericks: Return
  to Whitehorn
ΔThe Bachelor Bet

Previously published under the pseudonym Robin Elliott

Silhouette Special Edition

Rancher's Heaven #909
Mother at Heart #968

Silhouette Intimate Moments

Gauntlet Run #206

Silhouette Desire

Call It Love #213
To Have It All #237
Picture of Love #261
Pennies in the Fountain #275
Dawn's Gift #303
Brooke's Chance #323
Betting Man #344
Silver Sands #362
Lost and Found #384
Out of the Cold #440
Sophie's Attic #725
Not Just Another Perfect Wife #818
Haven's Call #859

JOAN ELLIOTT PICKART

is the author of over seventy novels. When she isn't writing, she enjoys watching football, knitting, reading, gardening and attending craft shows on the town square. Joan has three all-grown-up daughters and a fantastic little grandson. In September of 1995, Joan traveled to China to adopt her fourth daughter, Autumn. Joan and Autumn have settled into their cozy cottage in a charming, small town in the high pine country of Arizona.

THE MACALLISTERS

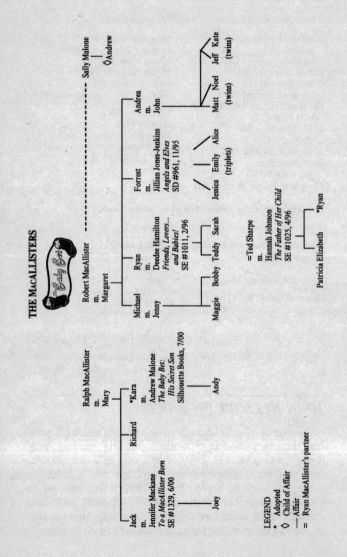

The Baby Bet Co.

Robert MacAllister m. Margaret ----- Sally Malone

◊ Andrew

Ralph MacAllister m. Mary

Richard — Jack

Michael m. Jenny

Ryan m. Deedee Hamilton
*Friends, Lovers...
and Babies!*
SE #1011, 2/96

Forrest m. Jillian Jones-Jenkins
Angels and Elves
SD #961, 11/95

Andrea m. John

*Kara m. Andrew Malone
*The Baby Bet:
His Secret Son*
Silhouette Books, 7/00

Jennifer Mackane m. Jack
To a MacAllister Born
SE #1329, 6/00

Andy

Joey

Maggie — Bobby Teddy Sarah

Jessica Emily Alice
(triplets)

Matt Noel
(twins)

Jeff Kate
(twins)

=Ted Sharpe m. Hannah Johnson
The Father of Her Child
SE #1025, 4/96

Patricia Elizabeth — *Ryan

LEGEND
- • Adopted
- ◊ Child of Affair
- ---- Affair
- = Ryan MacAllister's partner

Chapter One

Jennifer Mackane stretched leisurely, then snuggled deeper beneath the blankets on the bed with a sigh of contentment.

She wasn't scheduled to work today, or tonight, at Hamilton House, she mused, and would be able to spend the free hours with her precious Joey. They'd straighten up around the house and run errands, then indulge in dinner at Joey's favorite fast-food restaurant.

She'd have the luxury of tucking a fresh-from-his-bath Joey into bed that night and reading him a story as he drifted off to sleep. Bliss. Sweet bliss.

A faint aroma of freshly brewed coffee reached Jennifer, and she knew the automatic timer on the machine had produced the hot, beckoning brew.

No, she thought. She'd stay in bed a while longer,

be sinfully lazy. Then again, the coffee smelled so deliciously tempting.

"Oh, who am I kidding?" she said, laughing. "That coffee is calling my name."

She threw back the blankets and left the bed, poking her feet into enormous yellow slippers that boasted the head of a smiling Big Bird.

Joey was so proud of those slippers he'd given her for Christmas last year, she mused. He'd gone shopping with his Uncle Brandon and Uncle Ben, the outing producing the bizarre slippers as Joey's gift to his mom.

Jennifer had shot dagger-filled looks at Brandon Hamilton and Ben Rizzoli when she'd opened her present, and had seen the merriment and mischief dancing in their dark eyes. But she'd become accustomed to the pair's nonsense while the three of them had grown up together. Here in the pretty little town of Prescott, nestled high in the mountains a hundred miles above Phoenix, they'd enjoyed an idyllic childhood.

Jennifer thudded her way toward the kitchen as she smoothed her red flannel nightshirt down to her knees. Big Bird's heads bobbed up and down with each step she took.

Joey would be checking to see that she was wearing these silly creations, she knew, despite the fact that it was nearly a year since he'd given them to her.

In the large kitchen of the old, three-story Victorian house, Jennifer poured herself a mug of hot coffee, then opened the refrigerator to find the carton that would provide the splash of milk.

She hesitated and frowned, her gaze falling on the bridal bouquet on the bottom shelf of the refrigerator. She added milk to the coffee, retrieved the bouquet, then settled at the kitchen table, staring at the lovely flowers as she took her first sip.

She could clearly recall the shock and dismay she'd registered when the bouquet had come sailing through the air at Megan and Ben's wedding reception yesterday and somehow landed in *her* hands. She'd stared at it in wide-eyed horror, as the other women in the assembled group cheered for her, telling her she was now officially destined to be the next bride.

"No way," she had said, poking the flowers with one finger. "Not a chance."

She had planned to quietly slide the bouquet behind the stack of wedding gifts on the table at the reception and forget it. But Joey had been jumping up and down with excitement, declaring his mom to be a great pass catcher, just like whomever he had said caught the football from some quarterback he'd named. Joey had insisted on holding the touchdown bouquet all the way home.

Jennifer got to her feet, went to one of the cupboards and rummaged through it until she found a vase. She filled it halfway with water, then returned to the table and began to carefully dismantle the bouquet, sticking the flowers into the water.

They would now be just flowers in a vase, she decided, with no old wives' tale connotations connected to them. Not that she actually believed in the whoever - caught - the - bouquet - is - the - next - bride theory, but why take unnecessary chances?

She had no intention of remarrying, and having the bridal bouquet take up residence in her refrigerator even overnight was long enough, thank you very much.

"There," she said, admiring her work. "They're flowers in a vase, nothing more. The spell is broken. End of story."

"Hi, Mom," a sleepy Joey said, coming into the kitchen. He peered under the table at Jennifer's feet.

"Hello, sweetheart," Jennifer said, her heart warming at the sight of her sleep-rumpled, five-year-old son in his Rugrats pajamas. "How's my big boy this morning? Ready for some breakfast?"

"Guess so." Joey slid onto a chair opposite her, yawned, then frowned. "Whatcha do to the flowers you caught?"

"They needed water to stay fresh so we could enjoy them," Jennifer said.

"Oh. Well, you still get to be the next bride like everyone said. Can you have a chocolate wedding cake if you want to when you're the bride? Aunt Megan and Uncle Ben's cake tasted kinda yucky. You should pick chocolate for yours."

"Sweetheart," Jennifer said, "I'm not going to have a wedding cake because I'm not getting married."

"Yes, you are," Joey said, his voice rising. "Everyone at the party said so after you caught the flowers. You'll be a bride like Aunt Megan was and…well, first you gotta find somebody to be the groom guy, then I'll have a daddy like Sammy. That's how it works, Mom. It does."

Jennifer felt a chill sweep through her and tighten into a cold fist in her stomach.

"Joey," she said gently, praying her voice was steady, "you've never said you wanted a daddy. We're a team, you and me, the two of us. We're doing great together, don't you think?"

"Yeah, sure, Mom, but..." Joey shrugged. "It would be nice to have a daddy like Sammy does. They do men stuff together."

"Well, you do...men stuff with Uncle Ben and Uncle Brandon, and even Uncle Taylor when he comes up from Phoenix. They take you fishing, camping, hiking—all kinds of things."

"Yes, but..." Joey sighed.

"But what, sweetheart?" Jennifer said, leaning toward him.

"When I'm done doing men stuff with Uncle Ben, and Uncle Brandon, and Uncle Taylor, I have to give them back. I don't get to keep them, Mom. I don't have a daddy all the time like Sammy does."

"I see," Jennifer said softly, struggling against threatening tears. "But you know that's because your daddy is in heaven with the angels, Joey. I can't change that, sweetheart."

"You could be a bride like you're supposed to be 'cause you caught the flowers," Joey said, nearly yelling. "All you need is a guy to wear a suit and tie and buy you a yellow ring like Uncle Ben got Aunt Megan. How come you won't do that, Mom?"

"Joey, I realize that you don't understand and that you're getting angry at me because you don't. When you're older, bigger, this will make sense to you."

Joey scowled and dropped his chin to his chest. "No, it won't."

Jennifer stared at her son, her heart aching.

She had known, somewhere in the back of her mind, that this discussion would take place one day, she thought miserably.

When Joey was three years old, he'd asked why he didn't have a daddy, but had readily accepted the explanation that his father was in heaven with the angels.

Now, at five years old, Joey was comparing his family to that of his best friend, Sammy, and deciding it came up very short.

She'd worked so hard at being both mother and father to her son, and was eternally grateful to Ben, Brandon and Taylor for stepping in as father figures for Joey whenever they could.

But now her little boy wanted his *own* daddy, just like Sammy had. His uncles just weren't enough.

Oh, Joey, I'm so sorry, Jennifer thought, blinking back tears. What he wanted, she would never give him. She could not—would not—marry again. All she could do was weather this emotional storm of Joey's and hope, pray, it would soon pass.

Added to that heartfelt prayer was the ongoing one that Joey would never learn the truth about his father. *No one* knew the true facts of her past with Joe Mackane, and, heaven help her, no one ever would.

"Well," she said, forcing a cheerful tone into her voice, "you must be a hungry boy. How would you like pancakes made in the shape of animals?"

Joey's head popped up. "Yeah. Cool. I want a horse and elephant and hippopotamus."

Jennifer laughed and got to her feet. "A hippopotamus? Goodness, I don't know if I'm that talented a pancake artist, my sweet, but I'll give it my best shot."

Joey slid off his chair. "I'll pour my own milk into a glass. I need milk for my bones and teeth."

"Indeed, you do, sir," Jennifer said, taking a bowl out of a cupboard. "You'll grow up big and strong like...like your uncles."

And be a fine, upstanding man like your uncles, with no hint of the lack of morals and values of your father, she mentally tacked on, as she began to prepare the pancake batter.

Joey looked so much like her—it was as though Joe had had nothing to do with the child's creation. Joey had her wavy, strawberry-blond hair and fair complexion. His eyes were a sparkling green, and his features resembled hers. Anyone could tell that he was her son.

No, there was no hint of Joe Mackane in Joey, thank God, and there never would be as she continued to teach him the important lessons of integrity and honesty. Ah, yes, honesty. That was definitely something Joe never possessed, nor knew the meaning of.

Joe had been killed in a construction accident a week before Joey was born. In heaven with the angels? Jennifer mused. No, not even close. He wouldn't have begun to qualify for admission. But that was something her son would never know.

* * *

After cleaning the kitchen after breakfast, during which she'd received a passing grade for her pancake hippopotamus, Jennifer showered and dressed in jeans and a green sweater that matched her eyes.

While Joey was putting away scattered toys in his room, Jennifer opened the drapes on the windows in the living room, then frowned.

There was a man standing on the sidewalk in front of the house. He was tall, extremely handsome, with dark, auburn hair, rugged features, wide shoulders, and long, muscular jeans-clad legs. His hands were shoved into his jacket pockets, and he was staring at the top of the house, apparently unaware of her sudden appearance in the window.

What was he doing there? Jennifer wondered. Who was he? If he was a thief casing the place, he wasn't being very subtle about it.

All right, he had two minutes to be on his way, or she was going to march out there and confront him.

Jennifer narrowed her eyes.

Maybe that was dumb. Friendly, small-town Prescott or not, it was probably foolish to demand an explanation from a perfect stranger.

Perfect? Well, on a score of one to ten, the man was an eleven as far as looks and build went—but that was beside the point. She was a woman alone with a small, vulnerable boy to protect.

No, she'd give it another minute, then call Sheriff Montana and tell him about the stranger who was still—darn him—scrutinizing her home, her safe haven. He would handle this in the proper manner.

Okay, buddy, she thought, it's now one minute and counting.

Jennifer's breath caught as her gaze connected with the stranger's. He smiled, sketched a salute, then spun around and walked down the sidewalk.

A frisson of heat coursed through her and settled low in her body. She wrapped her hands around her elbows, then moved to the edge of the window, watching until the man disappeared from view.

Dear heaven, she thought, that smile of his should be registered as a lethal weapon, along with the loose-limbed, oh-so-sexy way he walked.

It had been many years since she'd had a sensual response to a member of the opposite sex. It was unsettling, to say the least, and very unwelcome.

It was also borderline crazy. She'd had a physical reaction to a man she didn't even know, and who might very well be a thief contemplating breaking into her house to steal her worldly goods, such as they were.

What on earth was the matter with her? she thought, shaking her head. On that horrifying day of Joe's funeral, when she'd learned the truths that had shattered her world, she'd begun the process of building a wall around herself.

Never again, she had vowed, would a man awaken her sexuality. Never again would a man touch her heart or her body. Never again would she love someone who was capable of destroying her.

"Mom," Joey yelled, running into the room, "I found my favorite dinosaur. It was under my bed. Cool, huh?"

Jennifer drew a steadying breath, then turned to smile at her son.

"Very cool," she said. "Oh, it's very dusty, too. Let's wash it off in the kitchen sink. There's nothing worse than a dusty dinosaur."

That evening, Jennifer settled onto the sofa in the living room in front of the crackling fire in the hearth, and picked up the mystery novel she was in the process of reading. Joey was fast asleep, having nodded off during the tale of *Peter Pan.*

She tucked her legs up close to her on the puffy cushion, spread an afghan she had knitted across her lap, and opened the book to the page that boasted a brightly colored bookmark Joey had made her for Mother's Day.

After reading one sentence, the image of the stranger who had stood in front of her house that morning superimposed itself over the words on the page.

"Darn you," she said, snapping the book closed. "Would you just go away and leave me alone?"

She sighed and shook her head as she set the book next to her, then stared into the leaping flames of the fire.

The anticipated, carefree day with Joey had been a disaster. Everywhere the two of them had gone, she found herself looking for that man, while at the same time registering excitement and fear.

The stranger had haunted her through the seemingly endless hours of the day. And with the thoughts of him came the disturbing remembrance of the rush of heated desire that had suffused her when he'd smiled.

"Oh-h-h, I'm driving myself crazy," Jennifer said aloud, throwing up her hands.

Okay, enough of this, she admonished herself. She was getting a grip right now. She'd analyze this bizarre behavior of hers, figure out why she was acting so unlike her norm, then be done with it.

"Fine," she said, tapping one fingertip against her chin. "Wait...a...minute. Of course. That's it."

She was the victim of a series of events that had taken place in rapid succession.

First, she'd attended the beautiful wedding of her dear friends, Ben and Megan, who were obviously deeply in love.

While she had neither the intention nor the desire to remarry, the romantic event had no doubt poked a bit at her subconscious and emphasized the lack of a special man in her life—even though she didn't want one...

Second, she'd caught the wedding bouquet, and had been surrounded by people declaring over and over that she would soon fall in love and be the next bride.

Third, Joey had expressed his sadness over not having a father, which had made her heart ache for her son.

If one added up all those events that centered on romance, love, a husband, a daddy that Joey wouldn't have to give back...well, it was no wonder she'd overreacted the very next time a handsome man directed a smile at her.

Thank goodness, she'd figured it out. She felt so

much better. It was amazing what a little inner dialogue could do to get a person squared away.

With a decisive nod, Jennifer picked up the book, found her place on the marked page and began to read.

Just before four o'clock the next afternoon, Jennifer entered Hamilton House, the hotel where she was manager of the dining room.

The beautiful building had been completely restored by her childhood friend Brandon Hamilton, after he'd dropped out of the fast lane in New York and returned to his roots in Prescott.

The large lobby was exquisite, transporting a person back to the turn of the 19th century. The Victorian furnishings, the original cabbage-rose carpeting, the gleaming piano by the front windows— everything was perfect.

Along the far wall was a simulated old-fashioned, cobblestone street, complete with lampposts to light the way. Open-fronted specialty shops beckoned to be explored.

One of the shops, Sleeping Beauty, offered feminine apparel and luscious bath accessories. The store was a smaller version of the one in Phoenix that was owned by Taylor Sinclair's wife, Janice.

Jennifer waved at Ryan, who was on duty behind the reception desk, then headed down the hallway that led to the dining room.

For the next hour, Jennifer was busy as she checked the reservation book for the evening ahead, spoke with the dinner and pastry chefs, reviewed and approved an order the wine steward wished to place, and conferred with the manager of house-keeping regarding the condition of the high-quality, linen tablecloths and napkins that were used in the dining room.

At five o'clock she was at her post behind the podium by the doors, ready to welcome the first guests arriving for dinner.

The flow of patrons moving in and out kept her bustling back and forth as she sat the guests at their tables and presented them with oversize menus.

A little after seven o'clock, Jennifer returned to the podium yet again, then smiled automatically as the doors to the dining room opened.

And then she stopped breathing.

Her smile disappeared, her eyes widened and her heart began to beat in a wild tattoo.

It was him, she thought frantically. *The man.* He was now beyond magnificent, in a dark blue sport coat over a white shirt and blue tie, and gray slacks. But it was most definitely him.

The stranger who had stood on the sidewalk in front of her house and might very well have decided on the best method to break in.

The man who had smiled at her, causing a desire to swirl within her, and who had haunted her thoughts ever since.

Dear heaven, what was he doing here? Had he followed her? Was *she* the reason he had studied her house? Was she being stalked by a raving lunatic?

Jennifer looked quickly around the room. What should she do? Scream at the top of her lungs? Grab the receiver to the telephone on the podium and call Sheriff Montana?

No, no, she had to calm down. She was surrounded by people, was safe...for the moment, at least. She'd just bluff her way through this until she could formulate a sensible plan.

"Good evening," she said to the man, unable to produce even the smallest smile. "May I help you?"

Jack MacAllister walked slowly toward the podium, his gaze riveted on the woman who had spoken to him.

It was her, he thought incredulously. The beautiful lady in the window of the intriguing Victorian house.

The woman who had not been far from his mental vision ever since he'd seen her yesterday morning as he'd stood on the sidewalk in front of her home.

She was even more lovely up close. Her eyes were green—incredibly green, and her hair was a silken tumble of strawberry-blond waves to just above her shoulders. Her features were delicate, her lips made for kissing. What he could see of the pale green dress she was wearing gave hint of lush breasts beneath the soft material.

And for some unknown reason, she was staring at him as though she expected him to leap over the podium and strangle her with his bare hands.

All he had done was walk into the dining room of the hotel, but, heaven only knew why, he was scaring this breathtaking feminine creature to death.

He'd never caused *that* kind of reaction in a woman before.

"Good evening," he said, stopping in front of the podium and producing his best, hundred-watt smile.

"I apologize if I startled you when I opened the doors."

"Startled me?" she said, more in the form of a squeak.

"Well, yes—I mean, you look rather...frightened."

"Frightened?" She splayed one hand on her breasts. "Me?"

"Look," Jack said, frowning as he extended one hand toward her, "I don't know what I did to—"

She took a step backward. "Don't come any closer. I might appear frightened, but I'm not. No, sir, not one little bit. I'm wise to you, mister. I have a great many friends in this town, including the sheriff, and you'll never get away with it—not in a million years."

"Huh?"

She glanced quickly around the room. "Just—just..." She flapped one hand at him. "Shuffle off to Buffalo. Get out of Dodge. Give up on whatever your diabolical scheme is before you end up in the clink."

"Huh?" Jack said again, totally confused.

"Hey, there you are," a deep voice said.

"Brandon—" Jack and the woman said in unison.

Brandon Hamilton strode to the podium. "Jennifer, I'd like you to meet Jack MacAllister, a good buddy of mine. Jack, this lovely lady and I have been friends since before we could walk and talk. This is Jennifer Mackane."

"It's a pleasure to meet you, Ms. Mackane," Jack said, grinning.

Chapter Two

Before Jennifer was forced to respond to Jack MacAllister's greeting, the dining room doors once again opened.

When she saw Brandon's wife, Andrea, and his great-aunts, twin sisters Prudence and Charity, enter the room, she nearly flung herself at them for a group hug.

"Hi," she said weakly, then snatched up a pile of menus. "Your table is ready. Let's go." She shook her head slightly. "I mean, would you follow me, please?"

Rushing from behind the podium, she bumped smack-dab into Jack, and the menus went flying in all directions.

"Oh, I'm terribly sorry, Mr. MacAllister," Jennifer said, not looking directly at him. "My, my, clumsy me. I'll just pick these up and—Brandon, you have the corner table by the windows. I'll be with you in just a second.''

Jennifer squatted to collect the scattered menus, only to have Jack hunker down next to her and retrieve two of them.

''I'll give you a hand,'' he said.

Jennifer's head snapped up, and she found herself only inches from Jack. He was looking directly at her, a small smile on his lips.

Chocolate fudge sauce, she thought. That was the color of Jack MacAllister's eyes. Delicious, chocolate fudge sauce. Good grief, he was handsome—so ruggedly male, as though his features had been chiseled from rough stone.

There were tiny lines by his eyes, and she guessed he was maybe thirty-five or thirty-six. His hair was thick, an auburn shade reminding her of a glossy Irish setter.

His nose was straight, his jaw square, his lips masculine but soft, as though waiting for a kiss....

Jennifer, get a grip, she ordered herself, averting her eyes from Jack's. There was that heat again, that damnable heat, swirling low within her, pulsing, causing a warm flush to stain her cheeks.

Jennifer stood, clutching the menus to her chest. Jack rose and offered two more to her.

''Thank you,'' she said, nearly snatching them out of his hand. ''Brandon, why are you still here? I thought you were going over to your table.''

''We will, sweetie pie,'' Aunt Charity said, ''just as soon as we figure out what in the blue blazes is the matter with you.''

"Yes, dear," Aunt Prudence said. "You do seem a teeny bit flustered this evening. Is something wrong?"

Jennifer looked at the elderly aunts. Although they were twins, their mirror image was the only similar thing about them.

Aunt Prudence was wearing a sedate gray dress with a high neck and long sleeves. Aunt Charity was decked out in yards of royal blue taffeta, the dress reminiscent of a turn-of-the-19th-century dance hall costume.

Andrea was standing next to tall, dark and handsome Brandon. Her maternity dress was peach, which accentuated her lovely, silky dark hair. She had an expression of concern on her pretty face.

"I'm fine," Jennifer said, producing a passable smile. "I just overreacted to something I shouldn't have overreacted to, that's all. My imagination got the better of me and...I'm fine now."

"Hold it," Jack said, snapping his fingers. "The lightbulb just went on over my head. You saw me on the sidewalk in front of your house yesterday morning. *Staring* at your home. Casing the place, one might think. Am I getting this straight? Then I showed up here, and that scared the bejesus out of you. Right?"

Jennifer lifted her chin. "That's correct, Mr. MacAllister. Your behavior unsettled me. I apologize for..." She frowned. "No, I don't. I had just cause to question your intentions."

"You betcha," Aunt Charity said. "There was a stranger gawking at your house, for mercy's sake. That would shake up any single, unmarried, unattached, not-even-dating-anyone woman who has a little boy to protect."

"Thank you for sharing, Aunt Charity," Jack said, smiling at her.

"Just stating the facts, hotshot," Aunt Charity said, obviously pleased with herself.

Jennifer closed her eyes for a moment and squeezed the bridge of her nose as she drew a deep breath and let it out slowly. Then she raised her head and forced a smile into place.

"Welcome to the dining room of Hamilton House," she said, looking at a spot above the assembled group. "May I show you to your table?"

Jack chuckled. "Why certainly, Ms. Mackane. Do lead on."

"Call her Jennifer," Aunt Charity said. "She's a member of our family, and so are you now, Jack. Jennifer, call Jack...Jack."

"That's Jack MacAllister," he said, grinning at Jennifer. "Not Jack the Ripper."

"Mmm," she said, glaring at him.

Jennifer marched across the room to the designated table. When the others joined her, she shoved the stack of menus at Brandon, who grabbed them before they fell to the floor again.

"Enjoy your dinner," Jennifer said, then hurried away.

Everyone settled into their chairs, and Brandon passed out the menus.

"MacAllister," Brandon said, laughing, "you've only been in town a couple of days and you've already caused trouble. New York City is probably celebrating your permanent departure, and the citizens of Ventura, California, are shaking in their shorts.''

"Hey, I'm innocent," Jack said. "All I was doing was admiring a dynamite example of historical architecture—which is badly in need of some tender lovin' care, by the way. I didn't intend to shake up the lovely Jennifer. She sure has a temper to go along with that red hair of hers.''

"She's a handful, all right," Aunt Charity said, peering at her menu. "Has been ever since she was a little girl. It would take a very special man to be a match for our Jennifer.''

"And a father for Joey," Aunt Prudence said.

"I assume Jennifer is divorced," Jack said.

"No, dear," Aunt Prudence said. "She's a widow. Her Joe was killed in a construction accident a week before Joey was born. Jennifer returned to Prescott to raise her son. Her parents relocated to Phoenix shortly thereafter due to Jennifer's mother having severe arthritis. Jennifer is living in their family home.''

"It's a lovely house," Andrea said, "but it's an awful lot for Jennifer to keep up, I'm afraid.''

"I see," Jack said slowly. "How old is Joey?"

"Five," Aunt Charity said. "He's cute as a button. Looks just like his mama.''

Jack frowned. "That's a good many years to mourn a man, no matter how great he might have been. Aren't there any eligible bachelors in this town?''

"Oodles," Aunt Charity said. "Jennifer seems determined never to remarry. Heaven knows, we've done our darndest to fix her up with the cream of the crop around here." She paused. "Maybe we should leap into action again, Pru. After all, Jennifer did catch Megan's bouquet at the wedding."

"Indeed, she did," Pru said, smiling.

"Oh, man, here we go again," Brandon said, chuckling. "Poor Jennifer."

"Sounds to me like the lady knows her own mind," Jack said. "She likes being single. End of story. The same holds true of me. All the match-making in the world wouldn't get me to change my stand on the issue. I'm a bachelor and intend to re-main one."

"Wanna bet, big boy?" Aunt Charity said, lean-ing toward him.

"You'd better shut up, MacAllister," Brandon said, shaking his head. "Aunt Charity and Aunt Pru are pros at this matchmaking bit. I was a confirmed bachelor, too, remember?"

"And so was Ben," Andrea said, smiling. "As well as Taylor."

"Yep," Brandon said, nodding. "And now we're all married. Don't get too mouthy on the issue, Jack. You never know what the future holds."

"I know what it holds for me on the subject of marriage," Jack said. "It ain't gonna happen."

"Yes, dear," Aunt Pru said, patting his hand. "We hear you."

"Ah, how the mighty will fall," Andrea said, smiling. "You did tell us the fascinating tale of the baby bet business that took place within the MacAllister clan, Jack. Your cousin, Forrest, was the reigning champion for eons—then *kaboom,* he was dethroned, so to speak."

"Yep," Brandon said. "That's how the story went. The same could hold true for the remaining eligible males in a bachelor bet. Look at how many of us have taken the fall." He glanced quickly at Andrea. "And very happily so, my sweet."

"Nice save, Hamilton," Andrea said, laughing.

"I'll be pleased to take your money in a bachelor bet, Brandon." Jack leaned back in his chair and crossed his arms over his chest. "So would my younger brother, Richard, I imagine. My sister is single, too, if you want to add bachelorettes to the soup."

"I want a piece of this action," Aunt Charity said, rubbing her hands together.

"I do believe," Andrea said thoughtfully, "that our new sheriff, Cable Montana, would be in the camp with you and your brother, Jack."

"The numbers grow," Jack said, nodding. "There are simply men in this world who have no intention of marrying…ever."

"I know," Brandon said, grinning at Jack. "I was one of them."

Jack flattened his hands on the table and leaned toward Brandon.

"The difference between us, buddy," Jack said, "is that I'll never change my stand on the issue."

"Yes, dear," Aunt Prudence said, smiling sweetly. "So you said."

Jack chuckled, sat back again and shook his head.

"You're all smiling like Cheshire cats," he said. "You obviously believe I'm full of hot air. Oh, easy pickings, that's what you are. Money in my pocket. How long before I can collect this bachelor bet? Do

I have to be a hundred and two and still single before you pay up?''

"We'll work out the details of that part of the bachelor bet later, big boy,'' Aunt Charity said. "Here comes our waitress. Let's eat. I'm starving to death while I'm sitting here.''

"So are we,'' Andrea said, patting her protruding stomach. "Baby Hamilton is doing gymnastics to let me know she's hungry.''

"She? She?'' Brandon said, raising his eyebrows. "Have you finally accepted the fact that I'm right? That we're having a girl? A daughter?''

"Sure, she has,'' Jack said. "I told you that when Forrest finally lost the baby bet, the baton was passed to the daddy-to-be. The fathers have been right every time since. If you say it's a girl, Brandon, then it's a girl. Your wife is a smart lady, and realized that the baby bet has proven itself. You're having a girl.''

"And smart person that I am,'' Andrea said, "I'm putting my money on your falling in love and losing the bachelor bet, Jack.''

Over the next hour, Jennifer carried out her hostess duties by rote.

She was furious at herself. She'd behaved like an idiot in front of Brandon's friend Jack MacAllister. Granted, she had just cause to have been frightened of Jack.

But then? Oh, good grief. Had she dismissed the incident as a misunderstanding, regained her composure and performed in a professional manner?

Oh, no, not her. She'd been caught up in a mishmash of lingering anger, along with acute feminine awareness of Jack's blatant masculinity. She'd turned into Ms. Fumble Fingers, dropping the menus, then added Shrew-of-the-Year to her titles while showing the group to their table.

Jennifer stepped behind the podium and stared at the reservation book, not really seeing the schedule of diners yet to arrive.

Even now, she thought, Jack MacAllister seemed to be somehow reaching out and touching her from way across the room. He was just so…there, and just so…male, and just so…

Heat feathered down her back, then wove into her to pulse low in her body. She shook her head in self-disgust, then looked at Jack from beneath her lashes.

Why? she wondered frantically. Why did that man have such a powerful and unsettling impact on her? He was just an ordinary man, for Pete's sake.

Well, no, that wasn't entirely true. She'd already conceded that Jack was an eleven on a scale of one to ten. He was so ruggedly handsome, so perfectly proportioned, and that thick, dark auburn hair of his was just begging to have feminine fingers sift through it.

And his eyes? Oh, those chocolate fudge sauce eyes mesmerized her and made it difficult to breathe.

Jennifer, stop it, she ordered herself, shifting her gaze back to the book. She was getting a grip—right now. All she had to do was bid Jack a pleasant goodbye as he left the dining room, and that would be that. She'd never see him again.

She frowned.

Wait a minute. Was he a guest at Hamilton House? If so, how long would he be staying in Prescott? Would he be popping into the dining room for dinner night after night? It stood to reason he'd be registered at his friend's hotel, but for how many days?

It didn't matter, she thought, lifting her chin. She'd been thrown off-kilter by Jack MacAllister for reasons she couldn't begin to fathom. But she was on full-alert now, her protective walls firmly in place. She was hereby immune to the spell-weaving Mr. MacAllister, even if he smiled that knock-'em-dead smile of his.

And the minute she got home tonight she was throwing away the flowers from Megan's bridal bouquet. Unsuperstitious or not, she wasn't taking any more chances.

Very good. She was back in control. Everything was fine. Thank heavens all of this ridiculous nonsense was at an end.

Jack listened absently as Aunt Charity related a tale of Brandon, Ben, Taylor and Jennifer's mischievous deeds when they were children growing up together in Prescott.

Ah, here we go, he thought. Some people had just entered the dining room, which meant—yes, there it was…Jennifer's smile. It lit up her face and caused those marvelous green eyes of hers to sparkle to the point where he was dazzled from across the room.

He'd watched her move through the tables with elegant, natural grace. She was femininity personified, and the heat throbbing low in his body told him that he was very aware of that fact, both mentally *and* physically. The fascinating Ms. Mackane was turning him inside out.

Which didn't make one bit of sense.

Jennifer was the type of woman he steered clear of, big time. She was, as the saying went, encumbered—with a five-year-old son, a home, a life-style that virtually shouted that the missing ingredients were a husband and father. No way. That was *not* his scene, not even close.

He'd also learned that Jennifer wasn't seeing anyone, wasn't into the singles' dating scene. She did not, therefore, know how to play the no-strings, no-commitment game.

Jennifer didn't wish to remarry, which was a point in her favor. A shaky point. He'd heard that bit before, but when a guy came along who collected a hefty paycheck, lo and behold, how quickly that tune could change.

Nope, he wanted no part of the lovely Jennifer. She was more than a pleasure to look at, was feisty and funny, and dynamite when she got her temper in a roar, but he would cut a wide path around her during the remainder of his stay in Prescott.

Jack watched as Jennifer led a couple to a small table in the center of the room. The man spoke to her, and Jennifer laughed as she handed the pair their menus.

A flash of heat rocketed through him as he heard the lilting sound of Jennifer's laughter. He shifted slightly in his chair and frowned.

Damn, he thought. Jennifer was pushing his libido buttons again. Why was she capable of doing that?

He controlled his actions and reactions toward women. *He* set the tempo, called the shots, and exited stage left at the first hint of possessiveness on the part of the woman in question.

He treated women with respect, showed them a good time, but he didn't particularly trust them.

He sure didn't know why Jennifer Mackane was able to hang him out to dry, but he'd had enough of it. She was upsetting his peace of mind and driving his raging body over the edge.

Why the hell was this happening to him—?

"Right, Jack?" Brandon said, snapping Jack back to attention.

"What?" Jack said. "Oh, sorry. I was off somewhere, I guess."

"She's thirty-three," Aunt Charity said, "but she looks younger, don't you think?"

"Who?" Jack said, an expression of pure innocence on his face.

"Give it up, hotshot," Aunt Charity said. "I've been sitting here watching you watching Jennifer through this entire meal."

"Me?" Jack said, raising his eyebrows. "Well, I may have glanced at her a time or two, but there's no harm in looking at the scenery, Aunt Charity."

"That's true, dear," Aunt Prudence said, "but you need to do more than look at our Jennifer. You should, as the gentleman I'm certain you are, speak with Jennifer privately and sincerely apologize for frightening her while you studied her home."

"I thoroughly agree," Andrea said decisively.

"Buy her some candy from the snazzy shop in

the lobby,'' Aunt Charity said, then paused. ''On second thought, buy me some, too. I love the stuff.''

''Hey, I didn't scare Jennifer intentionally,'' Jack said. ''It was a simple misunderstanding, that's all.''

''Which needs to be put to rest properly,'' Aunt Prudence said.

''You're dead meat, buddy,'' Brandon said, smiling. ''Don't argue the point any further, because you'd be wasting your breath. Apologize to Jennifer when you get the chance, and be done with it.''

''Mmm,'' Jack said, glaring at Brandon.

''What I was saying to you when you were daydreaming,'' Brandon went on, ''is that you're going to design our house while you're in Prescott. I was bringing the aunts up to date on that.''

''Oh. Sure. Right,'' Jack said, nodding. ''That's what I'm going to do, fantastic architect that I am. I'll have those plans to you and Andrea before I head to Ventura for the MacAllister reunion. Man, Christmas is going to be a zoo with the whole clan together.''

''It sounds like fun,'' Andrea said.

''I think the kids outnumber the adults by now,'' Jack said. ''The MacAllisters are into having babies, that's for sure. I'll have to learn how to talk to munchkin-type people, since I'm going to be part of the MacAllister architectural firm in Ventura. No more New York City rat race and brutal winters. Maybe I'll even learn how to surf.''

''You did the smart thing by leaving New York,'' Brandon said. ''I've never been sorry I dropped out of the fast lane.'' He smiled warmly at Andrea.

"Coming home to Prescott was the best thing I ever did."

"Thank you, love," Andrea said, matching his smile.

"Jennifer's hair is naturally curly," Aunt Charity said. "No fancy perms or globby makeup for our girl."

"Aunt Charity, would you cut it out?" Jack said. "I'm not interested in all the little details about your Jennifer. She has an interesting house that I'd love to do some restoration work on, and that's it. Period."

"I'm just chatting," Aunt Charity said, batting her eyelashes at him.

Jack shook his head and laughed.

"Maybe flowers would be a better gift of apology for Jennifer," Aunt Prudence said, pressing one fingertip to her chin. "Mmm. No, the chocolates are best, because Jennifer has fresh flowers at the moment. She caught the bridal bouquet at Megan and Ben's wedding."

"So you said," Jack said, rolling his eyes heavenward. "Which means Jennifer is to be the next bride and blah, blah, blah. I hope she'll be very happy with whatever guy she snags."

"That's the problem," Aunt Charity said. "We can't get Jennifer into snagging mode. Been working on that for years."

"So, it's settled, then?" Aunt Prudence said, leaning toward Jack. "You'll purchase some dainty chocolates for Jennifer?"

Jack raised both hands in a gesture of defeat. "Yes, I'll do it. I'll buy the bribe and humbly apologize to Ms. Mackane. Can we change the subject now?''

''Yep,'' Aunt Charity said. ''I'm ready for a sinful dessert. Bring it on.''

The dining room at Hamilton House closed at eleven o'clock, then preparations were made for breakfast the next morning.

Just before midnight, Jennifer turned off the lights, locked the doors to the dining room, then walked along the hallway to the quiet lobby of the hotel.

She waved goodbye to the clerk on duty behind the registration desk, then headed toward the front doors, buttoning her coat as she went.

As she passed one of the high-back chairs, a figure rose, startling her and causing her to gasp and stumble a bit.

''I'm sorry,'' Jack said. ''I didn't mean to frighten you.''

Jennifer frowned. ''Oh? You seem to be making it your life's work as far as I can tell.''

Jack closed the distance between them and extended a gold foil covered box toward Jennifer.

''My peace offering,'' he said, smiling. ''A token of sincere apology for upsetting you by staring at your house. Sweets for the sweet, and all that.''

Jennifer looked at the box, Jack's face, the box, then narrowed her eyes as she met Jack's gaze again.

''Aunt Pru and Aunt Charity put you up to this, didn't they?'' she said.

''Well…'' Jack said slowly.

Jennifer sighed and took the offered box of chocolates. "All right. So be it. I accept your apology, and the whole business is forgotten. You didn't have to stay up until midnight to do this."

Jack shrugged. "I'm a night owl." He paused. "May I walk you to your car?" *What?* he thought incredulously. *Where did that come from?* His intention had been to hand over the dumb candy, then head to his room and the soft bed that was waiting for him.

Jennifer laughed, and a bolt of heat shot through his body, causing him to frown at his now-familiar reaction to the lilting sound.

"You really don't want to volunteer to walk me to my car, Mr—Jack," Jennifer said. "It's parked in the driveway at my house. Thank you for the candy. My son, Joey, and I will enjoy it. Good night."

"Wait a minute," Jack said, as Jennifer started to move around him. "How are you getting home if you didn't drive to work?"

"I walked. Since you're so familiar with the location of my house, you know it's only a few blocks away, and the weather is surprisingly mild for mid-November in Prescott." Jennifer shrugged. "So, I walked."

"Are you nuts?" Jack said, his voice rising. "You can't stroll along the sidewalk at midnight. You'll get mugged before you go ten feet."

"I certainly will not," Jennifer said, matching his volume. "This is Prescott, Arizona, not…wherever it is you're from."

"New York City, and I don't care if this *is* cute

little Prescott. You've got no business walking home alone at this hour.''

''I do it all the time.''

''Well, you're not doing it tonight,'' Jack said, taking her elbow. ''Let's go.''

Jennifer jerked her arm free of Jack's grasp.

''You are, without a doubt, one of the pushiest, rudest men I have ever met,'' she said. ''You may be Brandon's friend, but that doesn't mean that *I* have to like you—which I don't. Good night, Mr. MacAllister.''

Jennifer marched toward the front doors of the hotel. Jack fell in step beside her, causing her to stop as she placed one hand on the door latch.

''Now what?'' she said.

''I'm going for a midnight walk, that's all,'' Jack said, smiling at her. ''If I happen to meander in the direction of your house...sue me.''

''You're really exasperating, do you know that?'' Jennifer said. ''Fine. Whatever. I'm not wasting any more of my time arguing with you. Your death, however, will not be on my conscience.''

''What death? I thought you said it was safe out there on the streets.''

''Oh, it is. However, you're not even wearing the sport coat you had on at dinner. This is not shirt-sleeve weather. If you get pneumonia and croak, it will serve you right.''

Jack chuckled. A shiver slithered down Jennifer's back as she heard the sexy, male rumble.

''I don't suppose,'' he said, ''that you'd wait while I went to my room for a jacket, would you?''

''Not a chance.''

"Didn't think so."

"End of story," Jennifer said, lifting her chin. "Goodbye."

Jennifer pushed open one of the doors and left the hotel.

Jack followed right behind her.

Chapter Three

The night was clear, crisp and incredibly quiet.

A million stars twinkled in the black-velvet sky, creating a silvery beacon to show the way as Jennifer and Jack turned the corner and left the lights of downtown Prescott behind.

Jack shoved his hands into his trouser pockets and hunched his shoulders against the chill as he matched Jennifer's long-legged stride along the sidewalk.

He was out of his tiny mind, he thought, mentally shaking his head. He probably *would* catch pneumonia and croak, which would be his just desserts for this ridiculous performance.

There he was, slowly freezing to death, as he escorted a woman—one who didn't wish to be escorted—home at midnight. Yep, he was definitely certifiably insane.

But…well, what could he say? A foreign sense of protectiveness had consumed him when Jennifer had announced she was about to walk home alone. There was no way he could just stand in the warmth of the hotel lobby and watch her set out on her own.

Oh, man, he was cold. He needed to do something to shift his attention from the fact that the blood was freezing in his veins. *So, MacAllister, talk to Jennifer.*

"Well, here we are," he said.

"Mmm," Jennifer said.

"Sure is quiet."

"Mmm."

"I'm used to New York, you know, the city that never sleeps."

"Mmm," Jennifer said again.

Jack sighed in defeat and trudged on.

Jennifer slid a glance at Jack, then looked quickly back down at her feet. She was being rude, she knew, by refusing to engage in the simplest conversation. But she just couldn't chatter like a magpie. Not yet. Not until she regained at least a modicum of control over her raging emotions.

She was acutely aware—again—that Jack's powerful male presence was causing heat to thrum within her despite the chill of the night.

But something more unsettling her now. When she'd realized that Jack intended to see her safely to her door even though he didn't have a jacket to wear, she'd had to struggle against very unwelcome tears.

Dear heaven, how long had it been…if ever…since she'd felt protected and watched over by a man?

How long had it been…if ever…since she had been made to feel special and important due to the actions of a man?

How long had it been…if ever…since she'd been able to relax and just be, because someone else had stepped in and taken charge?

Jack's stubborn insistence on walking her safely home had touched a place deep within her, and she'd been nearly overwhelmed by the emotions that gesture had evoked.

Oh, Jennifer, stop, she ordered herself.

Jack MacAllister wasn't Prince Charming riding to the rescue of a damsel in distress. He was a smooth operator who was accustomed to having his way with women, a man who rarely heard "no," she figured, from a member of the opposite sex.

They had engaged in a battle of wills of sorts, on the subject of her going home alone, and Jack obviously couldn't deal with losing the war. So there he was, freezing his tush off in order to proclaim himself the victor. What a dunce.

"Cold?" Jennifer said, glancing over at Jack.

He chuckled. "You'd better believe it. This was a pretty dumb thing to do, but my big-city instincts kicked in and… Well, I was obviously wrong. This town is buttoned down so tight, we haven't even seen a stray dog."

"You're admitting that I was right?" Jennifer said, surprise evident in her voice.

"Yep."

"Oh." She smiled. "Fancy that."

"What did you think? That I was on a big macho trip here? It's hard to be a hero when there aren't any dragons to slay." Jack laughed. "What I am is a six-foot popsicle."

Jennifer stopped walking, and Jack skidded to a halt.

"Jack, this is silly," she said, smiling. "Why don't you turn around and head back to the hotel. Jog or something to get there as quickly as possible. I appreciate your gentlemanly gesture here, but as you can see, it really isn't necessary."

"Hey, we're almost to your house," he said, matching her smile. "A jacket of Joey's obviously wouldn't fit me, but if I beg, maybe you'll loan me a blanket for my return journey in the wilds."

"I'd be happy to."

Jack nodded as he continued to look directly into Jennifer's eyes, now clearly visible in the silvery glow of the stars.

Neither of them moved. They hardly breathed. Time lost meaning. Heat began to curl and swirl within them, gaining force, pulsing low.

A sudden chill coursed through Jennifer, a wave of fear, of knowing she was losing control of the very essence of herself.

"No," she whispered, then spun around and hurried down the sidewalk.

Jack shook his head slightly to shake off the strange, sensuous spell that had been woven over him. "Man," he said, then took a much-needed deep breath.

He glanced quickly in the direction Jennifer had

gone, then sprinted after her, catching up as she turned onto the cobblestone walk leading to her house. She was fumbling in her purse for her key while holding the box of chocolates in her other hand.

"Jennifer—" Jack started.

"No," she said, going up the steps of the wide front porch.

She unlocked the door and entered the house with Jack right behind her. "I'll get you a blanket," she said, her back to him as he entered the house and shut the door behind him.

"Jennifer, wait a minute," he said. "We need to talk about what happened a minute ago."

She spun around, her green eyes flashing. "No, we do not," she said, her voice not quite steady. "There's nothing to talk about."

"But you felt it, I know you did. The heat, the pull, the—"

"Lust," she said, lifting her chin. "Let's give it the tacky title it deserves, shall we? That's what it was—lust. And as far as I'm concerned, the incident is forgotten. I certainly don't wish to discuss it."

Jack frowned, then shook his head slowly. "No, that wasn't lust," he said thoughtfully. "Nope. No way. I know lust when I'm caught up in it and that…whatever it was that took place between us was something very, very different."

Jennifer dropped her purse and the candy box onto the sofa facing the fireplace, where embers of a dying fire still glowed. Her coat joined the lot moments later.

"Whatever," she said, looking at Jack again.

"You have your opinion. I have mine. It really doesn't matter because the subject is closed."

"What are you afraid of?" Jack said, studying her intently. "I mean, hey, I'm a tad shook up myself here, because I've never experienced anything quite like that before. But I'm not *afraid* of it. I want to know what it was."

"Well, I don't," she said, wrapping her hands around her elbows. "Jack, please, let it go. It's late, I'm tired, and I have to be up early in the morning to get Joey ready for kindergarten."

Jack swept his gaze over the large room that was furnished with worn but comfortable chairs and a sofa. The tables were oak and had seen better days.

"Where's your baby-sitter?" he said.

"When I'm on this shift at the hotel, Joey sleeps at Mildred Clark's house next door. Mildred is a wonderful woman who is like a grandmother to Joey. In fact, he calls her Grandma Clark and… Oh, forget it. Why am I explaining all this to you?"

Jack smiled. "Because I asked?"

"Don't smile," she said, nearly yelling. "Don't you dare smile that smile at me."

"Huh?" he said, definitely no longer smiling.

Jennifer pressed one hand to her forehead for a moment. "I'm losing it. I really am. This is insane. I don't behave this way. What on earth is the matter with me?"

"Gotcha," Jack said, pointing at her. "See? You *do* want to know what that strange spell was that came over us out there in the cold, dark night. Whatever it was is what on earth is the matter with you. Get it?"

"What I'm going to get, mister," she said, "is a blanket for you. Then you are marching yourself out of here. Get it?"

"Got it."

"Good."

Jennifer nodded decisively, then left the room, returning minutes later with a blanket.

Jack burst into laughter. "You're kidding," he said. "You're sending me packing wrapped in a Winnie-the-Pooh blanket?"

"You'll be cute as a button," she said, shoving the brightly colored blanket at him. "Goodbye."

Jack tucked the blanket under one arm. "Okay. I'm gone. Lock up behind me."

At the door, Jack hesitated and turned. Jennifer was right behind him; their toes were nearly touching.

"I think—" he said quietly. "I truly believe…that you have the same questions and want the same answers that I do. It's all very confusing, don't you think?"

"I—"

"Shh."

Jack slid his free hand to the nape of Jennifer's neck, lowered his head and claimed her mouth with his.

Jennifer's eyes flew wide open in shock, but in the next instant her lashes drifted down as heat suffused her. Of their own volition her arms floated upward, then her hands encircled Jack's neck.

She savored the feel, the taste, the wondrous sensation of Jack's lips on hers, and offered no resis-

tance as his tongue slipped into her mouth to seek
and find her tongue.

Jack dropped the bulky blanket and gathered Jennifer close to his body, deepening the kiss as desire
rocketed through him. He raised his head a fraction
of an inch, then slanted his mouth in the opposite
direction, drinking in the tantalizingly sweet taste of
Jennifer. Heat coiled low and tight within him,
arousing him almost to the point of pain.

Jennifer, his mind hummed. He'd known, just
somehow known that it would be far, far more than
just a simple kiss. It would be ecstasy.

Jennifer was responding to him, holding nothing
back, returning his kiss with total abandon. He felt
ten feet tall because Jennifer was, in this moment
stolen out of time, his.

Jack groaned in pure male pleasure as he pressed
Jennifer even more tightly against him, relishing the
feel of her lush breasts being crushed to his chest.

Oh, his mind thundered, how he wanted her,
wanted to make love with Jennifer Mackane through
the remaining hours of the night.

The rumbling sound of Jack's sensual moan pen-
etrated the mist encasing Jennifer, bringing her back
to reality with a *thud,* jarring her from the rosy, sensuous place she'd floated to.

She broke the kiss, jerked out of Jack's embrace,
then took a shaky step backward as she drew a
steadying breath.

Jack shook his head slightly. "Whew. That was—
You are… Whew."

"That was," Jennifer said, hearing the thread of

breathlessness in her voice, "a mistake, should never have happened."

"Why not?" Jack said, frowning. "It was sensational *and* equally shared."

"I…" Jennifer started, then threw up her hands. "Yes, all right, I can't deny that I…took part in that kiss."

Jack smiled. "Kisses. Plural."

"Whatever," she said, hugging herself. "The fact remains that it—they, those kisses—were a mistake. I don't behave like this…ever. I don't know what came over me, but I'd appreciate it if you'd forget that this incident ever took place."

"Incident?" he said, raising his eyebrows. "Lady, it was a happening, an event, that defies description. Forget it? No way. Are you telling me that you can honestly *forget* how you felt, how you responded to me?"

"Yes. No. I…Jack, please, just go. I'm embarrassed and upset and— Just leave."

"Hey," he said gently, "don't be so hard on yourself. You're a young, healthy, beautiful woman, with wants and needs that are nothing to be ashamed of. We felt it—both of us. The desire—not lust, desire. There's nothing wrong with that."

"Yes, there is," she said, her voice rising, "because I don't want any part of feeling that heat, that need, that… No. I have no room for all that in my life—not anymore. Not now. Not ever again."

"Why are you doing this to yourself?" Jack said, matching her volume. "So, okay, you loved your husband, but, my God, Jennifer, it's been five years since that man died. He wouldn't want you to grieve for a lifetime, to cease to exist as a woman. You can't mourn him forever.''

"You don't understand.''

"No, I sure as hell don't,'' he said, restlessly raking a hand through his hair. "What I do understand—what I know—is that you want me as much as I want you.''

"No,'' she whispered, shaking her head.

Jack sighed in exasperation, then leaned down and grabbed the blanket from the floor. "I'm leaving now, Jennifer,'' he said, "but this discussion isn't over. There's something happening between us, and I want to know what it is. I'll be back.''

Jack turned and left the house, closing the door with a tad more force than was necessary.

Jennifer walked to the door on trembling legs, snapped the lock into place, then rested her heated forehead on the cool, smooth wood.

Dear heaven, she thought frantically, what had she done? She'd responded to Jack's kisses like some wanton hussy, had pressed her body to his, had felt his arousal surging full and heavy against her and had inwardly rejoiced in the knowledge that such a magnificent man wanted her. *Her.*

Sensuous images had flitted through her passion-laden mind of clothes disappearing by magic, of tumbling naked onto her bed and reaching eagerly for Jack, bringing him to her to fill her emptiness, to awaken her sleeping femininity with glorious lovemaking.

I'll be back.

Jack's fiercely spoken words echoed in her head, and she spun around, her eyes darting across the room in a near-hysterical search for somewhere to hide.

"To hide from Jack?" she said aloud, as tears stung her eyes. "No, heaven help me, to hide from myself."

This was her fault. She wasn't who she really was when she was with Jack. She didn't know why— just did *not* know why, but she *did* know she would be certain never to be alone with Jack MacAllister again.

Exhaustion swept over her like a heavy curtain, and she stumbled across the room, turning off the lights as she went. A short time later she slipped into bed, a weary sigh escaping from her lips as her head touched the soft, welcoming pillow.

Sleep. She needed to sleep, to escape from the turmoil in her mind, to put hours of distance between herself and what had transpired with Jack in her living room.

Sleep, she thought foggily. Then morning would come and everything would be fine in the light of the new day.

When sunlight tiptoed into Jennifer's bedroom the next morning and nudged her awake, she stirred, opened her eyes slowly...and thought of Jack.

With a muttered "Damn him," she threw back the blankets on the bed and stomped into the bathroom for her shower.

Dressed in jeans, a navy-blue sweatshirt and her Big Bird slippers, she entered the kitchen twenty minutes later in a less-than-chipper mood. With a mug of hot coffee in one hand, she began to assemble Joey's breakfast with the other, a frown on her face.

"Mom," Joey said, coming into the kitchen.

"What!" Jennifer snapped. Then her shoulders slumped. "Oh, Joey, I'm sorry. I sound like a grumpy bear. Good morning, sweetheart. Did you sleep well?" She paused. "How did you get into the house?"

"You didn't answer my knock at the front door, and the doorbell's broke, and I had to use the key from under the mat to get in."

Jennifer set her mug on the counter and lifted Joey into her arms. "I apologize," she said, then kissed him on the nose. "I didn't start my day with my best foot forward, but I'm fine now. I'll fix you breakfast, then walk you to school."

"'Kay," he said, wiggling to get down.

Jennifer set him on his feet.

"But don't hold my hand when we turn the corner by the school, Mom," Joey said, sliding onto his chair at the table. "That's baby stuff, and I'm big now."

"Yes, you certainly are getting big," she said quietly. "Very quickly, too. You'll be grown and gone before I know it."

Joey frowned. "Gone where? I belong here with you. I'm never going to leave you, Mommy. Never, ever, never. 'Cause if I did, you'd be all alone." He straightened in his chair and smiled. "No, you wouldn't. Not if you were the next bride 'cause you caught the flowers. Then you'd have a groom guy and you wouldn't be alone at all."

To Jennifer's dismay she was assaulted by the

memory of being held so tightly in Jack's embrace, wrapped in the safe, strong cocoon of his arms as he kissed her.

"Don't start *that* again, Joey. I am *not* going to be the next bride. I'll be just fine when I'm alone after you're grown up. Clear?"

"No," he said, sticking out his bottom lip in a pout. "I'm going to talk to Uncle Ben and Uncle Brandon about this. I'm going to tell them that you're breaking the rules about catching Aunt Megan's flowers. You told me I should never break rules, Mom."

"Oh, my stars," Jennifer said, rolling her eyes heavenward. "I don't believe this. We are now changing the subject. What do you want for breakfast? Cereal? Toast? Eggs?"

"Hot dog with mustard."

"Why not?" she said, throwing up her hands.

"And potato chips," Joey added.

"Don't push your luck, sir. I'll trade you potato chips for a banana."

"And orange soda."

"Milk."

Joey sighed. "'Kay."

Jennifer began to prepare the agreed-upon breakfast as Joey chattered about beating Grandma Clark at Candy Land the previous evening.

Jennifer laughed. "Poor Grandma Clark. You played Candy Land again? She can probably do it in her sleep by now."

"Huh?"

"Never mind."

"Guess what, Mom. It's my turn to feed the gerbil at school today. That is so cool. Can I have a gerbil of my own? I'll keep it in my bedroom.''

"Oh, ugh, no," Jennifer said, smiling. "Those things remind me of mice. Just enjoy the one at school."

"Can I have a dog? Know what? Sheriff Montana told me he might get a dog. If I had a dog, then my dog and Sheriff Montana's dog could be friends. Wouldn't that be really great?"

"One hot dog with mustard, plus a banana," Jennifer said, placing a plate in front of Joey. "There—you have a dog."

"That's a hot dog," Joey said, giggling.

"A dog is a dog. I'll get your milk."

Jennifer crossed the room and took a carton of milk from the refrigerator. As she turned again, she saw Joey jump from his chair. "Where are you going?" she said.

"Somebody is knocking at the front door," he said, running from the room.

"So early?" she said, frowning. "Wait, Joey. Don't open the—darn it."

Jennifer hurried after Joey as quickly as her Big Bird slippers would allow, the carton of milk still in one hand. Joey flung open the door, and Jennifer stumbled slightly before coming to a halt behind him.

"Hi," Joey said.

"Hi. I'm Jack MacAllister, a friend of your mom's. You must be Joey. I borrowed your blanket last night and I came to return it. I also brought some fresh cinnamon rolls from Hamilton House as a thank-you gift for allowing me to use your Pooh bear."

Jack shifted his gaze slowly to look at Jennifer. "Good morning, Jennifer," he said, smiling. "May I come in?"

"Sure," Joey said, stepping back and bumping into his mother.

Jack entered the house, and Joey slammed the door.

Jack swept his gaze over Jennifer, chuckling as he gave special attention to her feet. "Love the slippers," he said, grinning at her. "Milk? Great," he added, nodding toward the carton in her hand. "That will hit the spot with these cinnamon rolls. Come on, Joey. Let's dig into these goodies while they're still warm." He dropped the blanket onto the sofa.

As Joey and Jack headed for the kitchen, Jennifer just stood where she was, Big Bird slippers on her feet, a carton of milk in her hand.

"My life," she said, a rather bemused tone to her voice as she stared into space, "is suddenly out of control."

Chapter Four

Jennifer headed toward the kitchen, then stopped, staring down at her silly slippers.

She should make a detour to her bedroom, she thought, and change into her tennis shoes. No, forget it. Jack had already seen her funny feet, and besides, she'd never do anything to hurt Joey's feelings.

Joey, she thought, starting toward the kitchen again. He shouldn't eat one of those enormous cinnamon rolls from Hamilton House. He'd be on such a sugar rush, he'd be bouncing off the walls the entire morning at school.

"New York City," Jack was saying when Jennifer entered the kitchen.

"Wow. Cool," Joey said. "They have big apples there, or something."

Jack laughed. "Or something. But I'm moving to

Ventura, California. I just stopped off in Prescott to visit my buddy Brandon. I'm going to be a member of MacAllister Architects, Incorporated.''

"Why?" Joey said, then took a bite of the gooey roll.

"Why?" Jack frowned. "Well, because I was ready for a change, and it will be nice to be working with family."

"Whoa, Joey," Jennifer said, bringing a knife to the table where the pair sat. "Half a cinnamon roll for breakfast. You can have the rest later."

"'Kay," Joey said, as Jennifer cut the roll in two.

"You'll join us, won't you, Jennifer?" Jack said.

"I don't eat breakfast," she said, not looking at him. "A cup of coffee is all I have."

"Then bring your cup and sit down," Jack said.

"Yeah, Mom," Joey said. "You should do that because we have company."

"Mmm." She glared at Jack. "Very *early* company." She paused. "Oh, all right. Would you like some coffee, Jack?"

"Yes, thank you," he said, smiling. "Sounds great. I take it black."

"Dandy," she said, spinning around and nearly falling over her slippers.

Don't think, she ordered herself as she went to the coffeemaker. She would *not* entertain any thoughts, any memories—absolutely none—about what had happened between her and Jack the previous night.

She would not allow her bones to dissolve when Jack MacAllister smiled at her.

She would pay no attention to the flutter of heat that was now swirling and pulsing through her body.

She couldn't care less if Jack had removed his jacket to reveal a sweater that was the exact shade of his chocolate fudge sauce eyes.

She could handle this. No problem. Jack was just a man, who was sitting at her table stuffing his face with a cinnamon roll. A gorgeous man. A man whose shoulders looked a mile wide in that sweater. A sweater that encased strong arms that had held her so tightly, so safely in his embrace. An embrace that had included kisses that were ecstasy in its purest form and—

That's enough, she ordered herself. Get a grip.

She plunked a mug of coffee in front of Jack, retrieved her own from the counter, then poured a glass of milk for Joey. She sat down next to her son at the table and put the glass in front of him.

"Every drop, sweetie," she said.

"'Kay," Joey said, then looked at Jack again. "How come you had my Pooh blanket? Did you leave yours in New York City?"

"Something like that," he said, smiling. "I used your blanket like a coat, because I wasn't wearing mine and it was cold."

"Oh," Joey said, nodding. "Do you have a dog?"

"No," Jack said, then took a bite of roll. "Mmm. Delicious."

"Do you have a little boy?" Joey asked.

"No," Jack said.

"Do you have a wife lady?"

"No," Jack said.

Joey leaned forward. "Do you have a suit and tie?"

"Joey," Jennifer said quickly, feeling a flush of embarrassment heat her cheeks, "eat your breakfast. It's getting late."

"I have a suit and tie," Jack said. "Why did you ask me that?"

"Well, because you need to have a suit and tie if you're going to be a—"

"Time to go," Jennifer said, getting to her feet.

Joey glanced at the clock on the wall. "No, it's not. The big hand isn't at the top, Mom."

"Oh." Jennifer sighed and sank back into her chair.

"Back up, Joey," Jack said. "I'm definitely missing something here. I need to have a suit and tie to be a...what?"

"A groom guy," Joey said.

"Oh, good grief," Jennifer muttered.

"See, my mom caught Aunt Megan's wedding flowers and that means my mom is going to be the next bride, but she needs a groom guy if she's going to be a bride. Then I'd have a daddy I don't have to give back." Joey paused. "Just like Sammy has. See?"

"More coffee, Jack?" Jennifer said, looking at a spot about four inches above his head.

"No, I'm fine," Jack said, his gaze riveted on Joey. "Let me make certain I understand this, Joey."

"Oh, let's not," Jennifer said.

Jack ignored her comment. He leaned back in his chair and crossed his arms over his chest.

"I think I get the picture, Joey," he said, "except for the part where you have to give the daddy back."

"Oh," Joey said. "That's Uncle Ben, Uncle Brandon and Uncle Taylor. We do men stuff together, but…" He shrugged. "When we're done doing men stuff, I have to give them back."

"Ah," Jack said, nodding slowly.

"Sheriff Montana might be a good groom guy 'cause he's thinking about getting a dog," Joey went on. "But I don't know if Sheriff Montana has a suit and tie." He frowned. "The thing is, though, my mom doesn't want to be the next bride."

"Ah," Jack said again.

"That's breaking the rules of catching the flowers," Joey said.

"Indeed," Jack said.

"*I* can't break rules, so I don't think my mom should get to. Do you?"

"My, my, look at that big hand on the clock, Joey," Jennifer said. "Run and brush your teeth and get your jacket. Then I'll walk you to school."

"'Kay."

Joey hopped from the room on both feet, announcing that he was Tigger. As he exited, the coffee mugs jiggled and clinked on the table.

"That is one terrific kid," Jack said, smiling at Jennifer. "Man, he's neat."

"Yes, well, I think he's pretty special," she said, tracing the rim of her coffee mug with one fingertip. "He's all boy, that's for sure. Full of energy… Of course, as a typical five year old, he has definite opinions about things, and doesn't hesitate to express them. You have to discount a great deal of what he says because he has a tendency to blither on and on, whether he knows what he's talking about or not. Therefore—''

"Whoa," Jack said, raising one hand. "You've made your point. You want me to forget everything that Joey said about your being the next bride, and whether I have a suit and tie so I can be the groom guy. Right?"

Jennifer met Jack's gaze. "Yes," she said, nodding. "Joey has suddenly become obsessed with the idea that he wants a father. But he also wants a dog, so…" She shrugged. "This, too, shall pass."

"I don't know about that," Jack said seriously. "He seems pretty adamant about having a daddy. Uncles just aren't enough."

Jennifer sighed. "Having Brandon, Ben and Taylor spend time with Joey is the best that I can do."

"Is it?" Jack said quietly, looking directly into her eyes.

"Yes, it definitely is."

They continued to gaze at each other, and with the ticks of time came memories of the previous night. Memories of kisses shared and hearts racing. Memories of a soft body pressed to a rugged body. Memories of heated desire that licked throughout them like all-consuming flames.

Jennifer tore her gaze from Jack's and stared into her mug, willing her heart to quiet its wild tempo.

"Why did you come here this morning?" she said, not looking at him.

"To return the blanket. To meet Joey. To see if you were all right after last night."

"Of course I'm all right," she said, getting to her feet. "Because what happened last night is forgotten."

"Oh, come on, Jennifer, give me a break," Jack said. "You haven't forgotten it any more than I have."

"Believe what you wish," she said, starting across the room. "But you're not capable of reading my mind."

"No, I'm not," he said, "but I can sure as hell read what I just saw in your eyes a minute ago. Desire, Jennifer. Simmering desire."

Jennifer thudded her mug onto the counter and turned to glare at Jack. "Would you just leave it alone?" she said. "What happened was a mistake, should never have taken place. It's over. Done. Finished. Just forget it, Jack."

"No."

"Oh, you're exasperating," she said, throwing up her hands. "Fine. Don't forget it. I don't care. But I've erased it all from my memory bank."

"Is that a fact?"

"Yes," she said, lifting her chin. "It most certainly is."

"I see. You've totally forgotten how perfectly you fit against me when I held you in my arms? How it felt when I kissed you, and you returned those kisses in kind? You've forgotten the sensuous spell that comes over us whenever our eyes meet? You've forgotten that you wanted me as much as I desired you?"

"Stop it," Jennifer said, then glanced quickly at

the doorway that Joey had disappeared through. "Why are you doing this, Jack?"

He stood, then closed the distance between them. "I told you why. I want answers to the questions of what is happening between us. I'm an architect, Jennifer. I deal in facts, details. I don't like feeling confused. I don't rest until all the pieces to the puzzle are in place."

"And then you move on to the next challenge."

"Well—"

"I'm ready, Mom," Joey said, zooming back into the kitchen.

"Okay, sweetie," Jennifer said. "Say goodbye to Jack because he's leaving now."

"No, I'm not," Jack said. "I'll join you two on the walk to school."

"Cool," Joey said.

"No," Jennifer said.

"Why not, Mom?" Joey said, frowning.

"Yeah, Mom," Jack said, grinning. "Why not?"

Jennifer opened her mouth, hesitated, then snapped it closed again.

"Fine," she said, shaking her head. "We'll all walk to the school."

"Great," Joey said, jumping up and down. "Just like the three bears. Baby Bear, Mommy Bear and—"

"Joey," Jennifer said, "did you remember to put the cap back on the tube of toothpaste?"

"It doesn't have a cap, Mom. You bought me the push-the-button kind."

"Oh, so I did. I'll get my jacket."

Jack shrugged into his own jacket as Jennifer hurried from the room.

At the front door, Jennifer patted her pocket. "Okay, I have my house key," she said. "We're ready to go."

"It's none of my business," Jack said. "But…"

"What?" she said a tad sharply.

"Do you usually make this trek in the morning," Jack said, raising his eyebrows, "wearing your spiffy Big Bird slippers?"

Joey dissolved in a fit of laughter. And an embarrassed-beyond-belief Jennifer went to her bedroom to change into her tennis shoes.

The day was clear and crisp, the sky a bright blue dotted with puffs of white clouds. As the trio made their way along the sidewalk, Joey gripped one of Jennifer's hands and one of Jack's. The energy-filled child hopped on his right foot, then his left, then swung both feet in the air, using the adults as part of his human trapeze. Their combined laughter danced through the morning air.

Baby Bear, Jennifer's mind echoed. *Mommy Bear. And…Daddy Bear.* This was the type of outing she'd daydreamed about having someday with her husband and child. This was how it should have been, but hadn't been—would never be.

She glanced quickly at Jack, who was smiling down at Joey. Why had Jack insisted on joining her and Joey on the walk to school? she wondered. What sneaky motive did he have for making such an effort to be buddies with her son? What was Jack MacAllister after?

Good grief, listen to her. She sounded so hard, so bitter, so mistrusting. Well, fine. Better safe than sorry. She'd rather be squinty-eyed suspicious, than wide-eyed innocent and vulnerable.

She was, however, probably overdoing it a bit. Jack was on a vacation of sorts and was just filling idle hours. He was accustomed to the fast pace of New York City and was no doubt becoming bored in dinky Prescott. He had the opportunity to go for a walk with a cute, happy little boy and had decided to tag along with Baby Bear.

And Mommy Bear? her mind nudged. Did Jack see this stroll as a way to spend time with her, too? Yes, he probably did. He was determined, for heaven only knew what reason, to discover what was happening between them.

Why? Why should whatever was happening between them matter to a man like Jack? A man who could obviously have the amorous attention of any stunning, sophisticated woman who crossed his path.

Why? He was bored. That was it. She'd heard him telling Joey that he was on his way to Ventura to join the family architectural firm and had stopped in Prescott to visit Brandon. Jack probably hadn't realized this town was so small, but was too polite to cut his stay short.

So, he'd zeroed in on her for something to do? Oh, that was rotten. Really crummy.

Jennifer sighed.

There she went again, thinking the worst, drawing dark conclusions about men. She hadn't realized that was where her mind had settled during the past five years. Hadn't known, because Jack MacAllister was the first man in all that time to touch the woman within, to awaken the feminine part of her she'd put so firmly to sleep.

Oh, she didn't like this—not one little bit.

She didn't want to be awakened from her safe, protective slumber.

Nor did she wish to deal with the bitter, suspicious woman she was discovering she had become. A woman her husband's lies had made her.

Even more, she had no desire to acknowledge the...well, the desire itself that Jack had evoked within her—that incredible heat, that longing to mesh her body with his and make sweet, slow love for hours.

In short, she wanted to turn back the clock to before she'd seen Jack standing on the sidewalk staring at her house.

"One...two...three—" Joey yelled, then laughed in delight as Jennifer and Jack swung him through the air.

She was indulging in childish thinking, Jennifer's mind rushed on. She was doing a "Joey," could remember how he wanted to push the clock forward when he'd run out of patience waiting for his birthday to arrive.

She could *not* turn back the clock, any more than Joey had been able to move it forward. She *had* seen Jack, met Jack, been held and kissed by Jack. She had no choice but to deal with him.

And deal with him she would, by golly, by making it crystal clear, once Joey was safely deposited at the school, that she preferred not to spend any more time with one Mr. Jack MacAllister, thank you very much. There. It was settled, once and for all.

"Here we are," Jennifer said when they reached the school, she leaned down to give Joey a quick kiss on the cheek.

"Mom-m-m-m," he said. "Don't kiss me at school."

"Sorry," she said, smiling. "I lost control. I'll be right here by the gate to walk you home when the bell rings, sweetie. 'Bye for now."

"'Bye," Joey said. "'Bye, Jack."

"See ya, sport," Jack said.

"When?" Joey said.

"Off you go," Jennifer said. "You don't want to be late getting into your classroom."

"When will I see you again, Jack?" Joey said.

"Joey, the gerbil is hungry," Jennifer said. "It's your turn to feed him. Remember?"

"Oh, yeah. Cool. 'Bye."

Joey took off at a run across the schoolyard and disappeared into the building.

That little guy, Jack thought, was a heart stealer. Joey was so incredibly open and honest, he just stepped up and said whatever was on his mind. Kids were amazing, that was for sure, and Joey Mackane was extra special, no doubt about it.

What an awesome role it would be to be father to a child like Joey, a boy who would see his daddy as a hero and want to be just like him. Whew. Heavy stuff.

He'd never given much thought to being a father. Of course, it flickered through his mind now and again when he was with friends and family who had kids. But he'd always dismissed the idea out of hand, because with the child came the wife. The woman. The marriage. The commitment. The waiting to discover the *real* agenda of that feminine half of the partnership.

He'd been burned too many times by women who finally showed their true colors. The materialistic demands began. She wanted this, she wanted that...it never ended.

Oh, yeah—love me, love my paycheck, Jack thought dryly. Hell.

"Well," Jennifer said, bringing Jack from his thoughts, "Joey is all squared away for a few hours."

"Yep," Jack said, nodding. "He really is a neat kid, Jennifer. You should be very proud of the job you've done raising him alone."

"Thank you," she said, nodding her head slightly.

"So," Jack said, "what do you do after you've walked Joey to school?"

"Go to bed."

"Oh?" he said with a burst of laughter. "That sounds like it might be very enjoyable."

"Mmm," Jennifer said, glaring at him. "What I meant was, I go home and sleep for a couple of hours so I'm rested enough to enjoy the afternoon with Joey, then work the evening shift at the hotel."

Jack nodded. "Do you have other shifts at different times?"

"Yes, I rotate, and I have a schedule in place with Grandma Clark. Joey and I are so lucky to have her. My parents live in Phoenix because of my mother's arthritis. I grew up in the house where Joey and I are living.'' She paused. ''So, I'm off. Have a nice day, Jack.''

''I'll walk you home.''

''Are we back to my getting mugged on the wild streets of Prescott?''

Jack chuckled. ''No, we're back to I enjoy your company and I'd like to walk you home. I may even snag another one of those cinnamon rolls before I tuck you into bed.''

''I beg your pardon?'' she said, her eyes widening.

''Just kidding,'' he said, laughing. ''At least I know you're listening to what I'm saying. Some women smile and nod in all the right places, but they're actually thinking about the sale at Neiman Marcus, or whatever.''

''I've never even been inside a Neiman Marcus store,'' Jennifer said, starting down the sidewalk.

''But you'd like to be able to shop at a classy place like that,'' Jack said.

''That should have been a question, not a statement,'' she said, glancing at him as he fell in step beside her. ''The answer to the question would have been, I've never given it a thought. It's beyond my budget, so why dwell on shopping in stores like that?''

''Yeah, well, if someone handed you a credit card for Neiman Marcus, you'd manage to spend your share of the green stuff.''

''Nope,'' she said, shaking her head. ''I don't use credit cards. If I can't afford to pay cash for something, then I can't have it now.''

"You're kidding."

"No, I'm not, Jack."

"Amazing," he said, shaking his head.

"I don't know why," Jennifer said. "It makes very simple sense to me."

"But… Never mind."

"I get the feeling that you don't quite believe me, Jack."

"I didn't say that," he said. "I'm digesting what you said."

Jennifer shrugged, and they walked without speaking further.

Strange, she thought. She and Jack didn't know each other well enough for a sudden silence like this to be so comfortable. Yet it was. It was as though she'd known Jack for a long time, which was ridiculous.

Of course, nothing about her reactions to Jack MacAllister were even close to normal. Heavens, no. The sensual impact he continually had on her was absurd. Her incredible *awareness* of him was borderline insane, as was the quickening of her pulse each time he smiled that devastating smile of his.

And at the top of the This Is Nuts list was the fact that she'd returned his kisses with such heated abandon that the mere memory brought a flush to her cheeks.

Jack MacAllister was dangerous. Unsettling. Upsetting. Magnificent.

Oh, Jennifer, shut up, she admonished herself.

Jack chuckled suddenly, and Jennifer looked over at him questioningly.

"Groom guy, huh?" he said. "According to Joey, all it takes to be a husband is a suit and tie."

"Ah, the innocence of a child," Jennifer said, then sighed. "What a shame that Joey will have to travel the rocky road of adulthood. I'd like to wrap him in a cocoon and protect him forever, but I can't."

"No, you can't. Some people have rockier roads than others. Maybe Joey will be one of the lucky guys."

"I hope so. At least there are *some* tough truths I can keep from hurting him."

"Such as?"

"Oh, just…things. Here's my house. Do you want another cinnamon roll and cup of coffee?" Great, Jennifer thought, shaking her head in self-disgust. What had happened to making it clear that she didn't want to spend any more time with Mr. MacAllister?

"Sure. Thanks. Then I'll be on my way so you can get some sleep."

Jack followed Jennifer up the front walk leading to the porch. What truths was Jennifer determined to protect Joey from? he wondered. It hadn't been an idle statement on her part, because there had been a fierceness to her voice when she'd said it. She'd then avoided answering his question as to what she meant.

The lady had secrets.

Oh, yes, she was intriguing as well as desirable. There were many layers to Jennifer Mackane. She was like a mysterious, alluring package, waiting to be unwrapped to reveal what was within.

And for some unexplainable reason, he knew he wouldn't rest until he'd discovered who Jennifer Mackane really was.

Chapter Five

Jennifer cleaned up the kitchen after breakfast, while Jack treated himself to another cinnamon roll and a mug of hot coffee. He chatted about how he would be drawing the plans for Brandon and Andrea's dream house while he was staying in Prescott.

The couple had purchased a piece of land, he said, and had a contractor ready to get started. If the weather cooperated, the home could very well be completed by the time the Hamilton baby arrived in March.

Jennifer sank into the chair across from Jack, a dishcloth in one hand. "A new baby and a new home at the same time," she said wistfully. "Isn't that wonderful? Brandon and Andrea must be pinching themselves in an attempt to believe it's all true." She sighed. "Goodness."

"They're excited, all right," Jack said, nodding. "Now Brandon is bugging Andrea to decide on a name for their daughter."

"They know they're having a girl?" Jennifer said. "I wasn't aware of that. I thought Andrea had decided not to have an ultrasound."

"Ah, madam," Jack said, smiling, "you don't know the history of the MacAllister baby bet business. Brandon and Andrea qualify because they're close friends of yours truly—a MacAllister.

"Besides that, I have a cousin named Andrea over in California. Andrea MacAllister Stewart, to be precise, who is married to John. They have two sets of twins—Matt and Noel, and Jeff and Kate."

"My stars, they're busy parents."

"Yep. Anyway, Andrea Hamilton doesn't need a fancy test to determine if she is having a boy or a girl, because Brandon said a daughter is on the way, and so says the baby bet. It's a given."

"Wait, wait," Jennifer said, laughing. "I don't want to miss one word of this." She wiped up the table where Joey had been sitting, went to the sink to rinse out the cloth, then plunked back into the chair. "Okay, I'm ready. What's the scoop on the baby bet?"

Jack explained the famous MacAllister baby bet as Jennifer listened in delight.

"Such fun," she said, when he'd finished his tale. "It must be marvelous to be part of such a big family."

Jack nodded. "We sure had a lot of good times while we were growing up. I've been away for years living in New York, and I'm looking forward to being involved with the clan again.

"My folks retired to Florida, but they're flying in for the enormous MacAllister reunion that's being held at Christmas. That is going to be a zoo. Kids will be coming out of the woodwork."

"Super." Jennifer paused. "Well, you made a believer out of me. I'll buy some pink yarn and knit a blanket for baby girl Hamilton. I wonder what name Andrea and Brandon will pick for their daughter?"

"I don't know," Jack said, "but I hope between that project and the long list of decisions regarding the new house, they'll forget about the dumb bachelor bet nonsense they're talking about."

"This gets better and better," Jennifer said, laughing. "What's the bachelor bet?"

"Well, see, Brandon was a confirmed bachelor, as were your friends Ben and Taylor."

"They're all married now."

"Exactly," Jack said, nodding. "Brandon is yapping his head off about a bachelor bet, saying that I won't last at being footloose and fancy-free, and nor will my brother, Richard. There's someone else, too... Oh, yeah, the sheriff here in Prescott."

"Cable Montana?" Jennifer said. "The women in town are swooning over him, but as far as I know, he hasn't dated anyone since he moved here." She laughed. "Let me guess—Aunt Charity said she wanted in on the bachelor bet."

"Got it in one," he said, laughing with her. "She was rubbing her hands together, anticipating her winnings. Crazy people. What they haven't figured out yet is how old we have to be—and still single— before *we* can collect our money from *them.*''

''What a hoot,'' Jennifer said.

She leaned back in her chair and folded her arms beneath her breasts.

''So, you're a confirmed bachelor, huh?''

''In spades.''

''Why?'' she said, smiling and raising her eyebrows.

Jack chuckled. ''Why? You sound like Joey.''

''I guess I do,'' she said, her smile fading. ''Well, forget I asked, because it's none of my business. I don't intend to ever remarry, but I don't wish to get into a lengthy discussion as to why I feel that way.''

''I assume you're still mourning your husband, Joey's father.''

Jennifer shrugged.

Jack leaned toward her. ''I said it before and I'll say it again, Jennifer. Five years is enough—too long, in fact, to grieve for a man, for what once was. It's time to move on with your life. I realize that I'm overstepping here, but, damn it, Joey wants a father. Don't you yearn for a special man in your life?''

''No,'' she said firmly. ''I don't.''

''Damn,'' he said. ''You're one stubborn lady. You're making a tremendous mistake.''

''Oh? I do believe there is a double standard in effect here, Mr. MacAllister. It's apparently perfectly acceptable for you to be a confirmed bachelor, for reasons known only to yourself. But I'm making a big mistake by taking the same stance?''

''That's different,'' he said, frowning.

"Aha," Jennifer said, pointing a finger in the air. "One set of rules for men, another for women? Your mind-set is from the wrong century, Jack."

"You have a son to think about," he said, his voice rising.

"So I should marry the first thing that comes along in a pair of pants so Joey will have a father?" she said, matching his volume. "Not in this lifetime, mister."

They glared at each other for several long moments, then Jack smiled.

"What?" Jennifer said, still glowering at him.

"Who's going to be the groom guy in the suit and tie—the daddy bear—if you don't adjust your attitude?"

"Oh, good grief," she said, laughing in spite of herself. "This is so ridiculous. We're arguing like people who have known each other for a long time, when the truth of the matter is, we hardly know each other."

"Don't we?" Jack said seriously, his voice very low, very rumbly, and very, very male.

A whisper of heat slithered through Jennifer, and her smile disappeared. She was pinned in place by the sound of Jack's voice and the compelling depths of his chocolate-fudge-sauce eyes.

Memories of the kisses shared with him rushed over her. Her heart began to beat in a wild tempo, and the heat began to pulse low in her body.

Heaven help her, she thought frantically. She wanted this man with an intensity that was so frightening, it was like nothing she'd experienced in her entire life. She couldn't move, could hardly breathe and—

No.

She tore her gaze from Jack's and drew a trembling breath. She started to rise, praying her legs would support her, but Jack trapped one of her hands under one of his on top of the table.

"Jennifer, don't run from me," he said, his voice slightly husky. "Don't run from me, or from whatever it is that's happening between us. I would never do anything to hurt you."

Jennifer snapped her head up to look at him again, her green eyes flashing. She pulled her hand away from beneath his.

"Oh, really?" she said, an edge to her voice. "What a joke. You're passing through town. You see me as a challenge because I'm not falling all over you like your city women. So, what the heck, you'll keep after me until you get me into bed to satisfy your male ego and fill your idle hours, then go merrily on your way. But you would never do anything to hurt me? Give me a break, Jack."

Jack's jaw tightened slightly with anger and he narrowed his eyes. "I don't deserve that," he said. "You're making very unfair assumptions about me that aren't even close to being true."

He paused, then frowned as he studied her for a long moment.

"You're acting like a woman who has been...betrayed, terribly hurt, rather than like a widow grieving for the loss of perfection she had with her husband, the father of her son."

"That's enough," Jennifer said, getting to her

feet. "Now you're the one who is making assumptions."

Jack rose, met Jennifer as she came around the table, and gripped her shoulders. "Jennifer, wait a minute," he said quietly. "I don't want to argue with you. Let's back up. Okay?"

"Good idea," she said coolly. "We'll rewind this video to before you stood on the sidewalk staring at my house, then rewrite the script so that you walked down a different block and didn't have dinner at Hamilton House last night. Therefore, we never met."

"I wasn't thinking of reversing this scenario *that* far," he said, smiling. "You just erased me."

"Yep," she said, appearing quite pleased with herself. "I certainly did. Goodbye."

"Ah, but you're forgetting something," he said, his smile broadening. "It is a well-known fact that men in this country have a strange need to monopolize the remote control. It's in our genes or something. Therefore, *I'm* the one who decides where to halt this flick."

"Oh?"

"Indeed. I've pushed the button, and we are now back to last night in your living room and… Enough said."

Jack lowered his head and captured Jennifer's lips in a searing kiss that stole the very breath from her body.

No, no, no, she thought. *But… Oh, dear heaven, yes, yes, yes.*

She encircled Jack's neck with her arms and stepped into his embrace as he dropped his hands from her shoulders and wrapped his arms around her. He deepened the kiss even more, parting her lips, finding her tongue with his own.

Ah, Jennifer, Jack thought. It had been too long since he'd kissed her, an eternity since he'd been able to savor her sweet taste and aroma, the feel of her slender body pressed to his.

He'd never get enough of this woman; he needed, wanted more, much more. He was succumbing— very willingly at the moment—to the spell Jennifer was weaving over, around and through him.

He ached with the heated desire to make love with Jennifer Mackane.

Jack ended the kiss slowly, reluctantly, then sifted the fingers of one hand through Jennifer's silken hair as she rested her head on his chest.

They stood there, waiting for hearts to quiet and breathing to return to normal. They simply stood there, each lost in private, jumbled, sensual thoughts.

Then Jennifer sighed a sad-sounding sigh, a weary sigh that held the echo of tears.

"I can't do this," she whispered, still not moving. "I can't just listen to the needs of my body and ignore my emotions. I can't, Jack."

"I understand," he said, his voice hushed. "I won't push you, Jennifer, nor ask more of you than you're capable of giving. But I sincerely mean it when I say I want to know what's happening between us."

"Why is it so important to you?"

"I don't know. I guess because I've never felt,

experienced, anything like this before. It's so different, so...I want answers.''

"I don't."

"What are you afraid of, Jennifer?"

She sighed again. "Wakening what I've put so firmly to sleep...the essence of my femininity and all the wants and needs and driving, reckless actions that overpowering passion can result in. I can't. I won't."

"All right," he said, nodding slowly. "We have different agendas. I want the answers, you don't. You're in control of your—what did you call it?— the essence of your femininity. Okay. That's fine. You'll make certain that what is slumbering within you stays deeply asleep, no matter what I do or say. Am I getting this the way it is?"

"I, well... Yes."

He eased her away from him, and she lifted her head to meet his gaze.

"So, if I spent time with you," Jack went on, "in order to find my answers, to set things to rights within myself, it wouldn't upset you, hurt you in any way, because you have a firm handle on where you're coming from."

"Well, I don't know if—"

"Makes sense to me." He paused and nodded. "Sure, this is fine. So, I have a proposition for you."

Jennifer's eyes widened. "You what?"

"I'm not propositioning you in the way you're thinking," he said, taking a step backward and shoving his hands into his pockets. "What I'm hereby proposing to you will fall within the guidelines of what we've each determined to be where we are."

"You're losing me," Jennifer said, frowning.

"I need to spend time with you before I end up nuttier than a fruitcake trying to figure out why you're capable of weaving spells over me."

"I weave spells over *you?*" she said, splaying one hand on her chest.

"Big time. For all I know, it's a flash in the pan, and will burn itself out and be gone, *kaput.* I'll be back to normal. You'll be dandy while I'm hanging around because you've already cemented your program."

"Huh?"

"Hence, my proposition," he said. "This is one dynamite house that you live in."

"Now we're talking about my house?" Jennifer said, her voice rising. "I can't keep up with you."

"Pay attention. This house needs repairs, and my hands are itching to work on a historical structure like this one. You buy the supplies, I'll be the labor—free of charge."

"Oh, I don't think—"

"Good. Don't think it to death. Just agree. It's a win-win situation. I'll figure out why you've blitzed my mind and body, your house gets some tender lovin' care, and you're perfectly safe through the whole bit because your essence is asleep, or whatever. Get it?"

"Not really," she said, shaking her head slightly.

"Well, you're tired," Jack said. "Once you've rested, you'll understand the whole deal. I'll shove off so you can get to bed. We'll connect later so I can really have a go at examining this house. Then we'll decide which repairs have priority." He moved forward and dropped a quick kiss on her lips. ''See you later.''

Jack grabbed his jacket from the back of the chair in which he'd been sitting, then strode from the room.

Jennifer blinked, then frowned. That man, she thought, was like a steamroller operating at maximum speed. Had she just agreed to allow Jack to make much-needed repairs on her home? No, she certainly had not. Had she?

Jennifer sank back into her chair, the fingertips of one hand floating up to rest on her lips.

Oh, mercy, kissing Jack was wonderful. He made her feel so vibrantly alive, so womanly and desirable. She couldn't think rationally when he kissed her. She could only feel, savor—want more and more and more.

''Jennifer Mackane,'' she said with a sigh, ''you are treading in dangerous territory. What on earth are you doing?''

Well, she was grabbing a handful of...life. She was allowing her femininity to awaken and glory in its existence. She was filling her senses to overflowing with the taste, feel and exquisite male aroma of Jack.

And that was really, *really* dumb.

Jennifer plunked one elbow on the table and rested her chin in the palm of her hand. Well, maybe not *really* dumb, just borderline dopey.

Jack seemed to have a better handle on where she was than she did. He'd spelled it all out for her— how she couldn't be hurt by spending time with him because she was in control.

What was wakening within her, she could put back to sleep when she chose to do so.

That made sense. That was true. And that meant she could spend time with Jack, be held in his arms, be kissed by him, then bid him a breezy *adieu* when he left Prescott for his new life in California.

Kissed, she thought dreamily. Held in those strong, yet gentle arms. Make sweet, sweet love through the night with Jack MacAllister.

Jennifer sat bolt upward in the chair. ''Oh, now wait just a minute here,'' she said aloud.

Just how could she guarantee she wouldn't end up with a broken heart? She didn't have a clue as to the answer to that question.

All she could do was make certain she *was* retaining control of herself.

At the first hint that she might be growing more fond—yes, that was a good word—*fond* of Jack than was allowed within her emotional safety zone, she'd send him packing and resume her life as it had been before he entered her serene existence.

Her lonely existence.

No, no, now stop it, she admonished herself silently. She was alone, but not lonely. She had Joey, a challenging career, oodles of wonderful friends who were like a family to her.

But...

Yes, all right, sometimes, just once in a while, when Joey was asleep and the night stretched before her, she was a tad lonely. That was perfectly normal.

It didn't mean that she wanted a serious relationship with a man. And heaven knew she never intended to remarry. No, she just sometimes had the need to feel wanted and womanly.

And Jack was doing that.

Just for a while. Hours stolen out of time. Then he would be leaving town...and that would be that.

There was no way at all she could be hurt by any of this, because she was in control.

And Joey? She would make it perfectly clear to her son that Jack was here on vacation and would soon be leaving. Jack was *not* a potential suit-and-tie guy who would qualify to be a groom, a daddy bear. But Joey would benefit from another male influence in his life, even for the short term.

"Fine," she said, getting to her feet. Everything was hunky-dory, and the frosting on the cake was that her house was going to get some much-needed repairs.

She had absolutely nothing to worry about.

"Nap time," she said cheerfully as she left the kitchen.

Chapter Six

Jack settled onto a bench in the town square, then stretched out his legs and crossed them at the ankles. He unbuttoned his jacket to further enjoy the warming sun that was rising higher in the brilliant blue November sky.

He deserved an award, he thought, folding his arms over his chest, for having delivered some of the fastest talking blither ever produced by man. He'd rattled off his rationale to Jennifer without coming up for air, explaining why it was perfectly safe and sound for them to spend time together.

Why had he done that?

He'd been mentally scrambling, had been on the edge of panic that she'd tell him she didn't want to see him again. For reasons he couldn't begin to fathom, the idea of her sending him packing had caused a cold fist to tighten in his gut.

So, he'd steamrolled her, laid a bunch of malarkey on her, then hightailed it from her house before she had a chance to figure out what in the heck he'd actually said.

Why had he done that?

Jack sighed, shook his head, then dragged both hands down his face. He slouched lower on the bench and shoved his hands in his jacket pockets.

Actually, he mused, what he had rattled off to Jennifer wasn't all nonsense.

He *did* want to know what was happening between them. He didn't deal well with confusion and unanswered questions.

And no, he didn't wish, nor intend, to hurt her. If she was as in control of her emotions as she claimed to be, his presence shouldn't represent any potential harm to her mental health and well-being.

And yes, he really did want to do some repairs on that dynamite house of hers.

So, hey, what he'd said at warp speed had all been true. And to top it off in grand style, he would get to spend more time with neat little Joey.

Jack smiled as he replayed in his mind the earlier conversations with Joey.

"A groom guy," he said aloud, chuckling. "A daddy bear."

That kid was something. Cute. Smart. Knew who he was and what he wanted—a father. Well, according to Jennifer, Joey wasn't going to get one.

Jack narrowed his eyes.

Jennifer's adamant stance on never remarrying

was producing another slew of unanswered questions. There was something off-kilter there.

His assumption that Jennifer was still mourning her deceased husband was beginning to set off warning bells in his mind, indicating that there was a great deal missing from that picture.

Jennifer just wasn't coming across as a grieving widow. No, she seemed…angry—even close to bitter somehow. Why? What was the true story behind her marriage to Joe Mackane? She'd built strong walls around her heart, had put her femininity—or however she'd described it—to sleep, to be assured that no man would ever get emotionally close to her again. Why?

Why? Why? Why? Now *he* sounded like Joey.

Little heart-stealer Joey Mackane.

It was sure going to be tough saying goodbye to that nifty kid when it came time to head to California.

And the nifty kid's mother?

How would he feel when he walked away from Jennifer for the last time?

Sudden images of the kisses shared with Jennifer flashed through Jack's mental vision. The remembrances of her taste and aroma, of her being nestled against him, rushed over him, causing heat to coil painfully in his body.

"That's all," Jack said, getting to his feet. "Go for a walk, MacAllister. Don't think, just walk."

Jack spent the remainder of the morning in his room at Hamilton House working on the plans for Andrea and Brandon's house. He ate lunch with the couple in their apartment on the fifth floor of the hotel so he could show them what he had done and hear more of their ideas regarding their dream home.

"I love the lowered ledge near the ceiling in the kitchen," Andrea said, her eyes sparkling with excitement.

"It's called a pot wall, or sometimes it's referred to as a plant shelf," Jack said. "It gives you more of an opportunity to decorate a kitchen than you would normally have to make it uniquely yours."

"Perfect," she said.

"I'd like the back patio bigger," Brandon said. "We want room for the kids to play, plus be able to barbecue and eat out there."

"Got it," Jack said, nodding.

"Kids?" Andrea said, smiling at Brandon. "As in more than one?"

"Well, sure," Brandon said, matching her smile. "We'd spoil an only child rotten. Besides, she'd be lonely without a sibling to play and squabble with."

"Makes sense to me," Andrea said.

"At least she'll have a mother *and* a father," Jack said quietly.

"Why the serious expression?" Brandon said. "You grew up with a mother and father, Jack."

"I wasn't referring to me, Brandon," he said. "I was thinking about Joey Mackane. Do you know what he said? He likes doing 'men' things with his uncles, but it's not the same as having a father because...well, because he has to give the uncles back."

"Oh-h-h," Andrea said. "I'm going to cry. That is so sweet, but so sad. Poor Joey. He's obviously reached the age where he really misses having a father.''

"A daddy bear," Jack said, "to go along with the baby and mommy bears. He wants the whole nine yards, like his best friend Sammy has."

Brandon leaned back in his chair and crossed his arms over his chest. "Sounds to me like you've spent quite a bit of time with Joey," he said.

"And, therefore, with Jennifer," Andrea said. "They are, after all, a package deal."

"Don't get in a roar," Jack said, raising both hands. "I stopped by their house to return the Winnie-the-Pooh blanket, and took some cinnamon rolls with me for their breakfast. It's no big deal."

"Pooh blanket?" Andrea said.

"Oh, well, Jennifer loaned it to me because when I walked her home last night I wasn't wearing my jacket and it was a tad chilly."

"You walked Jennifer home last night?" Andrea said.

Jack frowned. "You're starting to sound like a parrot, Andrea, echoing everything I'm saying."

"Just gathering the facts, sir," she said, smiling brightly.

"Right," Jack said dryly, giving her a dark look. He shifted his gaze to Brandon. "What do you know about this Joe Mackane who Jennifer was married to?"

Brandon lifted one shoulder in a shrug. "Nothing. Jennifer and Joe were married somewhere in Colorado. A year or so later, Jennifer moved back to Prescott with a newborn Joey, after Joe was killed in a construction accident. None of us ever met Joe Mackane.''

"It's such a tragic story," Andrea said. "I can't imagine the horror of losing my husband, much less a week before our baby was born... I don't believe that Jennifer has ever really gotten over it. She refuses to even go out on casual dates, let alone remarry and give Joey the father he wants. She must have had a very special, very wonderful relationship with her husband.''

"Or a really lousy one," Jack said.

"What?" Brandon said, frowning.

"Think about it," Jack said. "You're all assuming that Jennifer's marriage was a match made in heaven. What if it was just the opposite? What if it was such a living hell that she has vowed never to get into a serious relationship with a man again?''

"You're forgetting something, Jack," Brandon said. "Jennifer named Joey after his father. A mother wouldn't do that if the guy was a louse.''

"She might do it as a smoke screen," Jack said, "to provide evidence that she had a happy existence with the man, when the truth might be the flip side of the coin. Does Jennifer talk about Joe? Relate stories about the terrific things they did together, shared as a couple?''

"No," Brandon said slowly, shaking his head. "She doesn't. She never mentions him, and changes the subject if someone brings up the topic of her marriage. We all assumed that it's too painful for her to discuss Joe.''

"After five years?" Jack said, his voice rising. "Come on, Brandon, get real. It doesn't add up.

Jennifer is too strong to be living that much in the past. It doesn't fit who she is.''

''You feel you know her that well to make that statement?'' Andrea said, raising her eyebrows.

Jack shifted his gaze to the pencil he was holding, fiddling with it as though it were the most fascinating thing he'd ever seen.

''Yeah, I know her that well,'' he said quietly. ''And I also know that something doesn't click here. Jennifer is definitely being influenced today by events that transpired in the past, but they're not necessarily memories of sweet bliss with Joe Mackane. Maybe I'm wrong, but I just don't think so.''

''Interesting,'' Brandon said, staring into space.

''It's also upsetting,'' Andrea said. ''The circumstances, the timing, of Joe's death were bad enough. It's even worse to entertain the idea that Jennifer's life with the man was a nightmare. Think of the pain she has bottled up inside her, if what you're saying is true, Jack. It's really heartbreaking.''

''This doesn't make sense,'' Brandon said. ''Jennifer has terrific parents, plus Ben, Taylor and I are like brothers to her. Andrea, Aunt Charity and Aunt Pru love her, too. Jennifer could have come to any of us and shared the truth about… No, I think you're out in left field on this, Jack.''

''Maybe Jennifer *did* confide in her parents,'' Andrea said.

''No,'' Brandon said, ''she didn't. Not with a negative story, anyway. Her father told me several years ago that it was obvious from Jennifer's behavior that no man would ever begin to be able to take Joe Mackane's place in her heart.'' He shook his head. "No, I just can't buy your theory, Jack."

"I could be wrong," he said, nodding.

"But what if you aren't?" Andrea said, leaning toward him. "If Jennifer doesn't deal with the pain of her past, she'll never experience the joy of a future with a special man."

Andrea paused and sighed. "How are we going to discover the truth, so that, somehow, if what Jack is saying is how it really is, we can help her?" she said.

"Don't look at me," Brandon said. "I don't have a clue. What are we supposed to do? March up to Jennifer and demand she spill the beans about her marriage to Joe Mackane? Yeah, right."

"No, the ticket is to pay attention to what Jennifer says and does," Jack said. "It's the little, subtle things that have given me the evidence I already have. The more I observe, the clearer the picture will be."

"That works for me," Andrea said. "Then, if it's really apparent that she is harboring dark, painful secrets, we could sit her down, explain that we love her, and offer to listen. Maybe if she talked it through, it would allow her to be free of it all, to move forward with her life."

"Just remember that Jennifer and Joe might have been so incredibly happy," Brandon said, "that she honestly doesn't wish to settle for less with someone else. I don't care if it's been five years or fifty since Joe died. If what they had together was close to perfection, then Jennifer has every right to live out her days with those memories."

"That's true," Andrea said.

"That stinks," Jack said, frowning, "and I don't believe for a second that Jennifer was on cloud nine with Mackane."

"Okay," Andrea said. "We agree that we don't know the truth. We agree that we care enough about Jennifer that we need to explore the issue further. The problem is...how? You said we should pay attention to the little, subtle things that Jennifer says and does, Jack. We're all busy people. We're not with Jennifer that often."

"*I* will be," Jack said.

"Oh?" Brandon said.

"I'm going to do some repairs on her house," Jack went on. "Jennifer will buy the supplies, and I'm free labor. Those kind of historical structures fascinate me as an architect. I'll report back to you, let you know if I discover anything of importance."

"A question," Brandon said, holding up one finger. "Why?"

"Why what?" Jack said.

"Why the interest in Jennifer?" Brandon said. "Why are you so concerned that she might be a...a victim of her past, so to speak? Why are you doing this?"

"That's none of our business, honey," Andrea said, patting one of Brandon's hands.

"It's not?" he said. "Yes, it is."

"No, it is not," Andrea said firmly. "If Jack has feelings for Jennifer, cares for her, realizes that she's a wonderful and special woman who deserves to be truly happy...well, that's none of our business."

"Hey, now wait a minute," Jack said. "I never

said I had *feelings* for Jennifer, or *cared* for her, for crying out loud. You're making this sound like a— a man and woman thing, when it's actually a…a…'' His voice trailed off, and he frowned.

"Yes?'' Andrea said, an expression of pure innocence on her face.

"It's…it's a humanitarian endeavor,'' Jack said. "Yes, that's what it is. I'm a nice guy who hates to think that a lovely, rare woman like Jennifer might be—what I mean is… Ah, hell, forget it.''

"Mmm,'' Andrea said, smiling sweetly.

"Do you want me to report back to you about what I learn or not?'' Jack said gruffly.

"Oh, of course we do,'' Andrea said.

Jack got to his feet and began to roll up the house plans. "I'm outta here,'' he said. "Jennifer is probably back home after collecting Joey from school, and I can take a look at her house. It was Joey's turn to feed the class gerbil today. He was really excited about it. Man, he's a neat kid.'' He paused. "Keep thinking about ideas for your house. Catch you later.''

"See ya,'' Brandon said.

"Goodbye, Jack,'' Andrea said. "And thank you for *everything*.''

"Yeah, sure.''

As Jack strode across the room, then left the apartment, Andrea folded her hands on her large tummy and smiled.

"This is *my* bedroom,'' Joey said, grabbing Jack's hand and attempting to hurry him forward. "It's neat-o.''

"You betcha it is," Jack said.

He swept his gaze over the all-boy room and nodded in approval. There was a bookcase constructed of boards painted in bright, primary colors and supported by cinder blocks. The shelves were jampacked with toys and books. Dinosaurs smiled from the bedspread and curtains, and model airplanes were suspended from the ceiling by ribbons. Joey's dresser was red with white pull-knobs.

"This is actually the parlor," Jennifer said. "My bedroom is in what should be the formal dining room with double doors. Since there's a full bath down here, I've closed off the upper floors to save money on the heating bills."

"Makes sense," Joe said, nodding.

"When I was a teenager," Jennifer went on, "I had the third floor all to myself. It's under the eaves, so when we go up there, you'll have to be careful not to bump your head." She laughed. "I used to pretend I had my own apartment. I felt so grown up and sophisticated."

"Can I live up there by myself when I'm big, Mom?" Joey said.

"Sure," she said, smiling at him. "You'll be able to talk to all your girlfriends on the telephone without me hearing you."

"I don't like girls too much," Joey said, wrinkling his nose. "They scream and holler when they see a worm, and they never want to get their clothes dirty. They just stand around and don't do nothing."

"Anything," Jennifer corrected automatically.

"That's what I said," Joey said. "They don't do nothing."

Jack chuckled. "Joey, my friend, I realize this is hard to believe, but you *will* change your mind about how you feel about girls."

"When you're twenty-five," Jennifer said quickly, causing Jack to hoot with laughter.

The trio completed the tour of the entire house, then Joey ran out into the backyard to play on his swing set. Jennifer and Jack went into the living room, where Jennifer sat in an easy chair, and Jack sat on the sofa.

"This really is a fantastic house," Jack said. "They sure knew how to design and build them way back when."

"It's lovely, but it's an awful lot to keep up," Jennifer said.

"Mmm," he said, nodding. "Well, my work is cut out for me, and I'm eager to get started. The stairs inside have dried out over the years and need repair. The shutters outside the windows are hanging on by a hope and a prayer. The front steps are sagging, as well as some of the boards in the porch itself. Then there's the—"

"Enough," Jennifer said, smiling. "Let's face it. My house is terminally ill."

"No, it's not. It just needs some tender lovin' care, and I'm just the guy to do it." Jack paused and looked directly at Jennifer. "I'm very good at tender lovin' care, Jennifer."

Jennifer's heart did a funny little two-step and a curl of warmth swept through her body. "Yes," she said softly, "I'm sure that you are…good at…" Her voice trailed off.

They continued to gaze at each other, assaulted by sensual memories as well as the heat of desire.

"Jennifer."

The sound of her name—*the simple sound of her name*—being spoken by Jack in a voice gritty with heightening want and need that matched her own caused Jennifer to shiver and tear her gaze from his.

"We agree, then?" Jack said.

Jennifer snapped her head around to look at him again, her eyes widening.

"To what?" she said.

To making love, sweet Jennifer, Jack thought rather hazily. Sweet, slow love for hours and hours—

He cleared his throat. "To my fixing up this place. You buy the supplies, and my labor is on the house—excuse the pun."

"Oh, yes, of course," she said. "And I appreciate it more than I can tell you."

"It will be my pleasure." Jack glanced around the room. "This home is a fine old lady."

Jennifer laughed. "Don't let Aunt Charity and Aunt Pru hear you call it an 'old lady.' They remember when it was built."

"Those two are something, aren't they?" Jack said, matching her smile. "They may be twins, but their personalities are as different as day and night." He paused and narrowed his eyes as he studied Jennifer. "They're on the same wavelength about one thing, though. Believing that everybody should be married. I gather they're really into matchmaking."

"Oh, they are, but they gave up on me several years ago, thank goodness."

"Don't be so certain of that," he said, still looking at her closely. "They're zeroing in on the fact that you caught that bridal bouquet."

"Good grief," she said, rolling her eyes heavenward. "Those flowers have caused me nothing but trouble. Joey got it in his head that since I caught the bouquet, all I need to do is find—"

"A groom guy," Jack finished for her, "who has a suit and tie. The daddy bear."

"I hope Joey won't make himself unhappy because he doesn't have a daddy like his friend Sammy. There are some things in this life that I just can't give him."

"Do you think that Joe Mackane would have been a good father to his son?" Jack said.

Jennifer averted her eyes and picked an imaginary thread from her jeans. "Well, I...I have no way of knowing that, do I?" she said, then sighed. "Yes, I do. Joe would not have been a— Never mind."

Dear heaven, she thought, what was she doing? She'd said enough that Jack now knew she didn't believe that Joe would have been a loving and devoted father to Joey. She'd never even hinted at such a thing to anyone before. Why now? Why Jack?

"I see," Jack said quietly. "How did Joe measure up in the husband department?"

Jennifer got to her feet. "I'd prefer not to discuss this further. Why don't I give you some money so you can shop for what you need to get started with the repairs? That's more efficient than my attempting to purchase what I don't know the first thing about. Good idea? Yes, it is. Certainly. Therefore—"

"Jennifer," Jack said, rising from the sofa. "I didn't mean to upset you by bringing up the subject of Joe."

"I'm not upset," she said, fidgeting. "I...I simply don't wish to talk about him. It serves no purpose."

"I agree," he said, nodding. "But his having an emotional hold on you serves no purpose, either."

"He doesn't," she said, her voice rising.

"Doesn't he?" Jack said quietly, starting toward her. "Well, that's very good news. That means that when I kiss you, you're kissing *me*. Not a ghost of another man. Me."

Jennifer watched Jack approach, trepidation, excitement and anticipation intertwining and tumbling through her.

He came closer...and closer...and...

Jack stopped in front of Jennifer, framed her face in his hands and lowered his head slowly, so very slowly, toward hers.

"Me," he said, then his mouth melted over hers.

Jennifer encircled Jack's waist with her arms as she returned the searing kiss in total abandon.

Kissing Jack, her mind hummed. Not a ghost of Joe. No, never that. Kissing Jack MacAllister. And it was heavenly.

The room disappeared as a sensual mist encased them, carrying them to a passion-filled place where they wished to stay, savor, want more, so much more. Heat pulsed and coiled and thrummed within them, heightening their desire to a near-frantic pitch.

A whimper of need caught in Jennifer's throat.

A groan rumbled in Jack's chest.

The back door slammed, and Joey's voice reverberated through the air. "Mom! Guess what!"

Jennifer and Jack jerked apart, then spun around to face the direction that Joey would appear. They each drew steadying breaths, willing their bodies back under control.

Joey ran into the room and came to a halt in front of the adults. "Mom," he said, then frowned. "What's the matter? You look funny."

"I do?" she said.

"Yeah." Joey cocked his head and looked at her intently. "Like when we run home from school. Your face is all pink and stuff."

"Oh, well, I guess I have the heat too high in here," Jennifer said.

No joke, she thought. She was on fire, desire still coursing throughout her. Dear heaven, her son had almost caught her kissing Jack, being held and caressed by Jack. This was terrible, just absolutely terrible.

"You went outside to play without your jacket, Joey," she said.

Joey shrugged. "You didn't tell me to put it on."

"You know you're to wear it in this weather," she said. "I shouldn't have to tell you." She sighed. "Remember next time. Okay?"

"'Kay. Guess what?"

"What?" Jennifer and Jack said in unison.

"I jumped off my swing from high up and didn't even fall on my butt. Great, huh?"

"Marvelous," Jennifer said, managing to produce a smile. "Just be careful when you do that."

"Jennifer, do you—" Jack started, then cleared

his throat when he heard the gritty quality of his voice. "Do you have a metal measuring tape?"

"Yes," she said. "Joey, would you get it for Jack, please? It's in the toolbox in the pantry."

"Sure," he said, then was off and running.

Jennifer turned to look at Jack, a deep frown on her face. "Do you realize what just happened?" she said, keeping her voice hushed. "Joey was seconds away from seeing us when we were..." She shook her head. "I can't believe that I was so irresponsible, so—"

"Human?" Jack said, matching her frown. "We weren't doing anything wrong, Jennifer. Joey is old enough to understand that you're a woman, as well as being his mother."

"Oh, listen to the child expert here," she said, planting her hands on her hips. "Joey is scouting around for a groom guy, remember? He'd believe he'd hit pay dirt if he saw us kissing. Get your suit and tie ready, MacAllister. Joey would have you signing on the dotted line to be the daddy bear."

"We'd just explain to him that people might kiss each other without having plans to get married." Jack nodded. "He's a smart kid. He'd understand."

"Wrong," Jennifer said, shaking her head. "You're very, very wrong."

"Got it," Joey said, zooming back into the room.

"Thanks, sport," Jack said, taking the measuring tape from Joey. "Let me ask you something, Joey. What does it mean when two people kiss each other?"

"Jack, for crying out loud," Jennifer said.

"You mean old people like you and Mom?" Joey said.

Jack chuckled. "Yes, old people. Not your friends at school."

"Oh, well, when old people kiss," Joey said, "they get a baby. I saw Uncle Brandon kiss Aunt Andrea when we all went on a picnic, and now they're going to have a baby." He frowned at Jack. "How come you don't know 'bout kissing and babies, Jack?"

Jack felt a foreign flush of heat creep up his neck, then glowered at Jennifer when she laughed.

"Yeah, Jack," she said. "How come?"

"I guess I forgot," he said. "Old people forget things sometimes."

"Oh-h-h," Joey said, nodding. "Well, if you forget something else, I'll tell you, 'cause I know a bunch of stuff."

"So you do," Jack said dryly.

"Do you want to kiss my mom and make a baby, Jack?" Joey said, jumping up and down. "That would be neat-o. You could be the groom guy, my daddy and—"

Jack reached out and planted his hand on Joey's head in mid-jump, causing the little boy to stop his pogo stick routine. "How would you like to help me measure some things, Joey?"

"Cool." Joey paused. "Why?"

"Why. Well, because I'm going to do some repairs around here. You know, fix what needs to be fixed."

"Sammy's daddy fixes up their house," Joey said. "That's daddy work."

Jennifer examined the fingernails of one of her hands. "Need a shovel, Jack?" she said pleasantly. "To dig yourself in a little deeper?"

"Could you help me out here?" he said.

"Nope," she said. "This is between you and Joey. Men stuff. You know what I mean? I'm going to see what's in the freezer that I can defrost for Joey and Grandma Clark's dinner. Have fun, you two."

As Jennifer left the room, Joey began to jump up and down again. "What are we going to measure first, Jack? Can I hold the tape? Can I pull it out? Can I tell you the numbers? Can I—"

"Sure, sure," Jack said, staring at the doorway Jennifer had disappeared through. "Whatever."

Had he just been set up? he wondered, narrowing his eyes. Had Jennifer very cleverly manipulated him into a scenario where he was once again a groom guy candidate in the eyes of her son?

Was one of her many secrets a hidden agenda to actually put the past behind her and snag a husband for herself, a father for Joey?

Did Jennifer have a well-thought-out master plan that he wasn't aware of?

That certainly would follow the rotten pattern of behavior of every woman—every damn one—he'd ever been involved with.

"Jack?" Joey said, tugging on Jack's arm.

"Oh. Right. Ready to get to work?"

"Yep."

"Could you get a piece of paper and a pencil from your bedroom?" Jack said.

"Yep," Joey said, then ran from the room.

No, Jack thought, looking at the empty doorway again. Jennifer wasn't like the others. Not Jennifer. She was real and honest, didn't play games. Not Jennifer.

Why not Jennifer? a little voice in his mind asked ruthlessly. She was a woman, wasn't she? Members of the female species were clever and sneaky, and always thinking, thinking, thinking.

Jennifer had a house that was badly in need of repair. And? Bingo. There he was, about to repair it. But that had been *his* idea. Hadn't it? Or had he somehow been made to *believe* that it was? Hell, he didn't even know anymore how the fix-it-up project came into being.

Man, oh, man, he was a muddled mess.

He'd sat in Brandon and Andrea's apartment and talked a blue streak to convince them that Jennifer wasn't necessarily being held in the grip of the past by memories of blissfully happy times with Joe Mackane, but possibly by remembrances of a disaster of a marriage.

Jennifer needed to let go of those ghosts and get on with her life.

But how did he know, how could he be really certain, that she wasn't already doing that? How did he know for sure that she, along with Joey, wasn't checking him out to see if he qualified to be the groom guy, the daddy bear?

Every woman he'd ever trusted had betrayed that trust with the revelation of what she really wanted. And it was never just him, the man, the person. Hell, no. It was what his money could buy said woman, the materialistic loot, the life-style she coveted.

Why should Jennifer Mackane be any different from the women who'd come before her?

But—but Jennifer was Jennifer and...

''Ah, hell,'' he said, dragging one hand over the back of his neck.

''You can't say 'hell' in our house,'' Joey said, reappearing at Jack's side.

''Sorry.''

''Here's a piece of paper,'' Joey said. ''I couldn't find a pencil so I brought a red crayon. Red crayons are good.''

''Fine,'' Jack said. ''I'm an award-winning architect who will be writing down measurements with a red crayon. Why the hell not? It makes about as much sense as the rest of my life at the moment.''

''You can't say 'hell' in our house,'' Joey repeated.

''Sorry,'' Jack said again. ''Be patient with me, Joey. I'm old, remember? Not only that, but I'm very, *very* confused.''

Chapter Seven

Jennifer stood by the front windows in the living room, watching Joey and Jack stack supplies close to the house on the grass near the edge of the sidewalk.

Joey had pleaded to be allowed to accompany Jack on the shopping trip, and Jennifer had finally agreed, with the stipulation that Joey wear his seat belt while riding in the vehicle.

With the pair's departure had come the silence within the big, empty house. With the silence had come niggling, negative voices in Jennifer's mind— voices that gained more and more volume—regarding her decision to spend time with Jack.

She sighed and shook her head. She was driving herself crazy. The longer Joey and Jack were gone, the more doubts she had that she could handle being in close proximity to Jack for the measured amount of days—and nights—he'd be in Prescott.

Fear that she was making a terrible mistake reached through her like icy tentacles. She could very well be playing emotional roulette, she concluded, and that was a very dangerous and foolish thing to do.

She had Joey to consider, too. She had to be concerned about his obviously growing attachment to Jack. She had to make crystal clear to her son that Jack was only in Prescott temporarily, then hope Joey wouldn't fantasize otherwise. Joey had to comprehend that when Jack left, they'd never see him again.

By the time she'd showered and dressed for work, Jennifer mused, still looking out the window, she'd done a complete reversal of her original decision.

She could not, would not, share any more desire-evoking kisses with Jack MacAllister. She had no choice as far as seeing him—the agreement regarding the repairs on the house was a done deal.

But she'd mentally place Jack in the same category as Brandon, or Ben, or Taylor. A brother type, a buddy, a pal. Jack would no longer be an attractive man, but a platonic friend.

As Jennifer stood there drinking in the sight of Jack, her heart was racing and the new familiar heat was pulsing in her body. She wanted to rush out the door and into his arms, feel his lips on hers, savor the power and masculinity of his magnificent body.

"Oh, Jennifer," she said aloud wearily, "make up your mind, would you, please?"

What she had to do was deliver, like a mantra,

the same speech to herself that she would give to Joey: Jack was here temporarily. Jack would leave. She would never see Jack MacAllister again.

And while he was in Prescott, she was going to grab a handful of life and live it to the maximum, rejoice in her womanliness, tuck each precious memory of what she shared with Jack safely away.

There, she thought dryly. She'd made up her mind. Again. Until when? The next time she was alone too long, the house was too quiet, the nagging voices in her mind spoke more loudly than her present resolve?

Oh, yes, she was definitely driving herself crazy.

As Joey and Jack started toward the porch, Jennifer went to the front door and opened it.

"Hi, Mom," Joey said, running into the house. "We got great stuff. Guess what? Jack bought me my very own hammer, 'cause I'm going to be his helper."

"Wow," Jennifer said, smiling at her excited son. "Your very own hammer. That's very special."

Jack entered the house, and Jennifer closed the door behind him. She gave him a quick smile, then redirected her attention to a chattering Joey, who was telling her in great detail about everything he and Jack had purchased.

Jack unbuttoned his jacket while his gaze was riveted on Jennifer. Beautiful, he thought. The burnt-orange dress she was wearing was a perfect color for her, and the simple style accentuated the womanly curves of her figure.

And her face as she listened to Joey! So open, so honest, so radiant with pure, motherly love.

How could he have doubted the *realness* of this woman? How could he have relegated her to the dubious ranks of all the other women he'd known? How could he have done such a crummy thing?

This was Jennifer, for heaven's sake, who was like no woman he had ever met before. She didn't have a sneaky agenda regarding him, wasn't after his money, his social status. Hell, no, not Jennifer Mackane. Sure, he'd just met this woman, but he *knew* her, deep down in his bones, in his heart.

"Well, I see you're ready for work," he said. "I'll take off and be back in the morning to get started on this place."

"I'll stay home from school so I can help you, Jack," Joey said.

Jennifer laughed. "Nice try, mister. You'll go to school in the morning, as usual."

"There's plenty to do around here, Joey," Jack said. "You'll get to use your new hammer as much as you want to, no doubt about it."

"'Kay." Joey sighed. "I guess."

Jennifer shifted her gaze to Jack. "Are you planning on having dinner at Hamilton House this evening?" she asked.

"No, Andrea wants Mexican food, says she's craving hot sauce, or whatever."

"Oh." For Pete's sake, she admonished herself. She'd felt it, the wave of disappointment that she wouldn't see Jack during the hours she'd be on duty in the dining room at the hotel. What a ridiculous, adolescent reaction.

"There are some great Mexican restaurants in town," she said. "I'm sure you'll have a delicious meal.'' She paused. ''Well, see you in the morning.''

''Right.'' Jack didn't move.

''Goodbye,'' Jennifer said.

''Right.'' He still didn't move.

''Jack?'' she said.

''Oh! Yeah, right. Have a nice evening. See ya tomorrow, Joey.''

'''Bye, Jack,'' Joey said.

Jack left the house and strode down the walk to his vehicle, parked at the curb. He got in and drove away, forcing himself not to look back at the house before it disappeared from his view.

He hadn't wanted to leave, he thought incredulously. It was as though his feet had suddenly become cemented to Jennifer's living room floor, making it impossible for him to walk out the door.

He didn't want to have dinner with Brandon and Andrea; he wanted to spend the evening at Jennifer's with her and Joey. They'd eat, clean the kitchen, play a board game or something, with Joey in front of a warm, welcoming fire in the hearth, then...

Ah, yes, then Joey would be put to bed and the remaining hours of the night would belong to Jack and Jennifer. He'd gather her into his arms and kiss her until they couldn't breathe. He'd see her incredible green eyes take on a smoky hue as her desire for him grew, along with his for her. Then they'd...

''Shut up, MacAllister,'' he said gruffly. ''Just shut the hell up.'' He paused. ''And remember that you're not allowed to say 'hell' in Jennifer's house.''

What a stupid scenario he'd just whipped up. Jennifer was on her way to work at Hamilton House. If he'd hung around, he would have ended up spending the hours with Joey, and watching Grandma Clark knit, or crochet or whatever, until she toted the kid to her house to put him to bed.

Man, he was losing it.

The MacAllister clan was in for a big surprise. When he arrived in California for the family reunion, they'd all discover that poor Jack was totally bonkers. They'd ship him off to the funny farm, never to be heard from again.

"That's where I'm headed, all right," he said, smacking the steering wheel with the heel of one hand. "Right over the edge of sanity."

Jennifer smiled as she waved good-night to the clerk behind the reservation desk, then slowed her step as she crossed the lobby of the hotel. She made a production out of buttoning her coat as she went, enabling her to slide glances at the high-back chairs to see if Jack was going to materialize and offer to walk her home.

As she fiddled with the last button, she finally accepted that he was nowhere to be seen. With a sigh, she left the hotel, admitting reluctantly the emotional letdown she was registering over Jack's absence.

She'd been disappointed when she learned Jack wouldn't be eating dinner in the dining room that evening. Now she was rapidly getting a full-blown case of the blues because he hadn't stayed up late to escort her home.

She was sinking below adolescent behavior. At

the rate she was going, she would end up pitching a screaming fit like Joey did on occasion when things didn't go the way he'd decided they should.

"Oh, me. Oh, my," she said aloud as she trudged along the sidewalk. Her life was suddenly so confusing and complicated. She had established a routine for her and Joey, an existence that varied little from one day to the next.

Week after week.

Month after month.

Year after year.

It was calm, predictable and...boring? Blah?

Lonely?

Well, she certainly hadn't thought so...until now. Until Jack.

But her mental condition was not entirely Jack's fault. No, the majority of her unrest was due to her own indecisiveness.

She'd decide that she was going to go for the sexual gusto with Jack while he was in town, then—*blam*—she'd get cold feet and vow not to see him again other than in a platonic relationship.

Jennifer continued to walk, her mind racing.

It was time to take a stand, to make a choice, then stick to it, before she worked herself into a complete nervous breakdown.

"Yes," she said decisively, then frowned. The problem was that she had no idea if she was going to take her firm stand on Plan A or Plan B. Darn, her mind was still running in circles as though she were a close relative of the gerbil in Joey's classroom, racing around in its never-ending exercise wheel.

"Get a grip, Jennifer," she muttered. "Get a brain. Get a life."

Ah, there was the key word. *Life.* Her life. The one she was suddenly questioning.

The mother part of her was filled to overflowing with her beloved Joey. He was her sunshine boy, who continually gave her so much, made her so complete and happy in her maternal role simply by being.

But the woman?

The woman wanted Jack.

With earthy, real, burning desire, she wanted to make love with Jack MacAllister, mesh her body with his, be filled with him, giving, receiving, becoming one entity as they savored the ecstasy of their intimate union.

Oh, yes, yes, yes, she wanted—

"Hello, Jennifer."

She gasped as she came to a sudden teetering halt in front of the steps to the porch of her house, having walked there by rote, not even realizing that she'd arrived home.

Jack rose in the shadows beyond the dim light cast by the lamppost at the curb. He had been sitting on the steps and now stood, tall and magnificent.

Jennifer spoke his name, vaguely aware that it would sound like a greeting, but knowing it was actually the conclusion of her sensuous thought.

"Jack."

"I'm sorry if I startled you," he said quietly.

"What are you doing here?"

"I need to talk to you," he said, his expression unreadable in the nearly total darkness. "I didn't want to insult your intelligence again by hanging around the hotel and offering to escort you safely home, so I waited for you here.''

''Oh. What—what did you wish to speak to me about?'' Jennifer said.

''Could we go inside?''

''Yes. Yes, of course.''

Jennifer retrieved her key from her purse and hurried past Jack, not looking at him.

She was flustered, she knew, and admonished herself for her ridiculous thought that she'd somehow conjured Jack up by having admitted how much, how very much, she wanted to make love with him.

She managed to draw what she hoped was an unnoticed steadying breath as she unlocked the door and entered the house with Jack right behind her.

Jack moved around her, and as she closed the door and turned to face him, he stepped in front of her, trapping her against the door, his hands on either side of her head. Jennifer's eyes widened in surprise, and the key and her purse dropped unheeded to the floor.

The glowing embers of a waning fire in the hearth cast a soft, golden glow over the room. Jack looked directly into Jennifer's eyes, and her breath caught as she stared into the depths of his eyes, those incredible chocolate fudge sauce eyes.

''We have to talk,'' he said, his voice low, ''because if I don't straighten out this mess called my mind, I'm going to lose what's left of my sanity.''

''I—''

''Hear me out,'' he said gruffly. ''Please.''

Jennifer nodded.

"You can't deny—or, at least, I hope you won't—that something is happening between us. One minute, I'm determined to discover what it is. The next, I have doubts about that being a smart thing to do. I bring my past into the present and decide to put a lot of distance between us before…but then I see you and I can't bring myself to do that. See? I'm going nuts."

"So am I," Jennifer said softly.

"What?"

"I want to run as far away from you as possible, Jack. I want to run into your arms. You terrify me because you're awakening a part of me that I vowed would stay asleep forever. Yet you excite me because you make me feel so vitally alive and womanly… I'm going crazy, too, and I can't go on like this. I just can't."

"I'll be damned."

"You can't swear in this house," Jennifer said, trying to produce a smile that failed to materialize.

"Sorry. Then we agree that we need to agree? What I mean is, we have to reach a decision about this situation that is acceptable to both of us?"

"Yes," she said. "Could we sit down?"

"In a minute. I'm thinking."

"I need to think, too, but I can't do that when you're so…so close to me because… Well, I just can't. This isn't fair, Jack. This conversation calls for clear and level heads."

"Yeah, okay."

Jack brushed his lips over Jennifer's, then stepped back to allow her to move away from the door.

Jennifer retrieved her keys and purse from the

floor, removed her coat and set everything on the back of the sofa. She waited until Jack had chosen to sit in one of the chairs by the hearth, then sat opposite him in another, the fireplace separating them.

"I should turn on a lamp," she said, starting to rise again.

"No, don't," Jack said. "I'll put another log on the fire."

The fresh log Jack put in place crackled, then caught fire. Both Jennifer and Jack stared into the hypnotizing flames, each lost in jumbled thoughts.

Jennifer shifted her eyes to sweep her gaze over the room, realizing that because of the brighter light in the hearth, the space beyond where she and Jack sat was now completely dark.

It was as though it wasn't there, she thought. All that existed was the glowing circle encasing the two of them in a golden hue. There was nothing beyond this space. Nothing. And for some unknown reason, there was a rightness about that—a peaceful sense of how it should be.

"Jennifer," Jack said, drawing her from her reverie. He leaned forward, resting his elbows on his knees and linking his fingers. "We agree that something is happening between us that is far from ordinary. We also agree that not knowing what to do about it is driving us both nuts."

"Yes," she said softly.

"Neither of us is interested in a serious, long-term relationship," Jack went on. "I'll be leaving Prescott in a month or so, and starting a new life in

California. We have a set length of time to be together, if we choose to be.''

''I'm aware of that.''

''Since we know all of this is temporary, there's
no way either of us can be hurt if we...well, I don't
mean to sound tacky...but if we go for it.''

''I understand what you're saying.''

''Good. I'm not forgetting about Joey, either,''
Jack said. ''We'd be sure to remind him that I'm
leaving before Christmas. We'll listen carefully to
what he says, be certain that he isn't fantasizing
about me being the groom guy or the daddy bear.''

''I'm glad you realize that Joey is an intricate part
of this—this decision,'' Jennifer said, smiling
slightly. ''That means a great deal to me.''

''Hey, he's a terrific kid. I wouldn't want to do
anything to upset him. Not ever.''

''Thank you, Jack.''

''Which brings us back to square one—the two
of us.'' Jack sank back in the chair and dragged a
hand through his hair. ''I'm so afraid that I'll present
this in such a way that it will come across as sordid
to you, when I know it wouldn't be. It truly
wouldn't.''

He stared up at the ceiling for a long moment,
then met Jennifer's gaze again. ''Okay, here goes,''
he said, then drew a steadying breath. ''Jennifer, I
want you. I want to make love with you. Holding
you, kissing you, is heaven itself, but I want more.
I ache for you, Jennifer.''

''I—''

''It's not lust, it's desire,'' Jack rushed on. ''Plus,
I enjoy being with you. You're complicated as

hell—oh, sorry—as heck, but you're fascinating, too, and fun, upbeat, and, heaven knows, you're beautiful.''

He smiled. "Actually, it was your Big Bird slippers that tipped me over the edge." His smile faded. "Am I making sense?"

"I—"

"During the weeks I have left here in Prescott, we could share so much," he said, as though she hadn't spoken. "All kinds of things. And during those weeks we'd be lovers, too. Then, when it's time for me to go, we'll each have memories. We won't be emotionally hurt by this, because we're being up front and honest about how things stand."

"I—"

"There you have it. I desire you more than any woman I've ever met. I've presented my case." Jack frowned. "I sure wish you'd talk to me, for crying out loud."

Get a life, Jennifer told herself. Feel beautiful, special, cherished and desired.

Awaken your essence for a few weeks, then put it back to sleep gently when time runs out.

No tears. No heartache. No pain.

Just lovely memories to relive in quiet moments when she was once again alone.

"Jennifer?" Jack said. "Say something. Please."

And so, she did.

With a soft smile on her lips and an inner sense of being incredibly and wondrously alive, Jennifer spoke.

She said one word that she knew would change

everything. She would never be quite the same again.

She said it with conviction, while trepidation hovered around the edges of her resolve.

She said it with courage that held a hint of fear.

She gazed directly into Jack MacAllister's mesmerizing eyes and said, "Yes."

Chapter Eight

Relief, joy, excitement and desire tumbled through Jack with such force that he was unable to sit still for one second longer.

He got to his feet at the same moment that Jennifer did, and they each moved forward to meet in front of the blazing fire.

Jack framed Jennifer's face in his hands and studied her intently. "Are you sure about this?" he said. "It's so very important that you're absolutely certain this is right for you."

"Oh, heavens," she said, smiling. "Reaching this decision was difficult enough without reexamining it under an emotional microscope."

"But—"

"Shh. No, don't." Jennifer's smile disappeared. "Jack, these weeks together will be like a gift I'm giving to myself, maybe selfishly so, but I intend to have this time with you. When it's over, when you leave, I'll be fine because I know this is temporary. It's perfect, really, because I'm not willing to commit myself to a permanent relationship.''

''I couldn't have said it better myself,'' Jack said. ''We're in complete agreement.''

Jennifer nodded.

''Good,'' he said, lowering his head toward hers. ''That's good.''

Jack captured Jennifer's mouth in a searing kiss, parting her lips and finding her tongue with his own. He dropped his hands from her face to encircle her body with his arms, and she melted into his embrace, wrapping her arms around his neck.

He raised his head a fraction of an inch to draw a quick breath, then slanted his mouth in the opposite direction as he claimed her lips once again.

The heat of desire burned within them. They were on fire, the want and need of each other consuming them.

They didn't think, didn't *need* to think, about the decision they'd made—not anymore. The turmoil of confusion was gone. They were free to just feel, savor, anticipate what was yet to come.

Jack broke the kiss, then murmured close to Jennifer's lips. ''I want you, Jennifer, so damn much.''

''Yes,'' she whispered. ''I want you, too, Jack.''

''Make love with me…here…by the fire.''

''Yes.''

They stepped back to allow room to shed their clothes, hurrying, the distance between them too great. Then they were naked, each standing still, allowing the other to visually trace every inch of what was within their view, what would be theirs.

"You're so lovely," Jack said, his voice raspy, "so beautiful."

"You're magnificent," Jennifer said.

Jack shook his head slightly to clear the sensual mist consuming his mind. "Wait," he said. "I want to protect you."

He fumbled with his jeans that lay on the floor and found his wallet, aware that his hands were trembling as he retrieved the foil packet. He returned as quickly as possible to Jennifer and drew her into his arms, kissing her deeply.

They sank onto the carpet in front of the crackling fire, stretching out next to each other. For a long, heart-stopping moment, they gazed into each other's eyes.

Then Jack lowered his head to claim Jennifer's mouth as he splayed one hand on her stomach, his weight supported on his other forearm.

He moved from her lips to one of her breasts, drawing the soft flesh into his mouth, laving the nipple with his tongue. Jennifer closed her eyes with a sigh of pure pleasure as sensuous sensations swept through her.

They kissed, caressed, explored, discovered the mysteries of each other, rejoiced in what was revealed to them. Lips followed where hands had traveled...and passions soared.

They were in a world that was only as big as the golden circle of light from the fire; a private world— their world—where no one else was granted entry.

It was ecstasy far beyond what either had ever known before.

"Jack, please," Jennifer said finally. "I need...please."

"Yes."

He moved over her and into her, slowly, watching her face for any hint of pain, knowing instinctively that it had been many years since her body had been filled with the very essence of a man.

Jennifer smiled. It was a soft, gentle, womanly smile...and Jack was lost. He thrust into her, bringing to her all that he was, and she received him in the moist heat of her femininity.

He began the rocking rhythm, and she matched him beat for beat in perfect unison. He increased the tempo, harder, faster, thundering, as they climbed higher and higher, reaching...reaching...

"Jack!" Jennifer said as she was flung into glorious oblivion.

He joined her there a second later, a groan rumbling deep in his chest.

They hovered, then floated back slowly. Jack kissed her, then moved off her, tucking her close to his side as he collapsed next to her, spent, sated.

"Oh, my," Jennifer whispered.

"Oh, yeah," Jack said.

"I've never felt so... There aren't words to describe how..." Jennifer smiled. "I think I'll just shut up."

Jack chuckled. "Okay." He paused and frowned. "I didn't hurt you, did I? It's been a long time since you've— What I mean is..."

Jennifer smiled at him. "I think *you* should just shut up."

"Good idea."

"Mmm," she said, her lashes drifting down.

"Don't go to sleep," Jack said, then yawned. "It wouldn't be too great if Joey came bouncing in the door in the morning and found us here."

Jennifer's eyes flew open again. "Don't even think such a thing. Jack, we must be very careful around Joey. He mustn't even see us kissing."

"No joke," he said, chuckling. "He'd tell the world that he saw us making a baby. Hey, you kiss, you get yourself a kid."

"Yep, that's how it's done," Jennifer said, laughing. She sobered in the next moment. "Joey is so innocent. I'd give anything to protect him from the world as it really is." She paused. "I suppose every mother feels that way."

"Some more than others." Jack rolled to his side, supporting his weight on his forearm so he could look directly at Jennifer. "It would depend on the mother's past experiences—if she'd been badly hurt, or had just sailed through life without having endured any emotional bumps and bruises."

"Mmm," Jennifer said, frowning.

"If the mother—that woman—" Jack went on, "was bitter, no longer trusted easily, she'd have to be careful that she didn't...I don't know... brainwash her child, make him wary of reaching out to people."

"I would never do that to Joey, even though—Never mind. It's getting awfully late, Jack.

I hate to end this wonderful night, but I have to get some sleep so I can function tomorrow.''

"Back up a minute," he said. "What were you going to say?''

"Nothing.''

Jennifer moved away from Jack, then got to her feet and began to gather her strewn clothes.

What was she hiding? Jack thought, watching her. He'd bet a buck it had something to do with Joe Mackane. Would Jennifer ever trust Jack enough to share her past with him?

Whether she did or not shouldn't matter, considering the temporary status of their relationship. They were living for the moment, with no plans for a future together. Their pasts held no importance in the overall scheme of things.

No, it shouldn't matter how deeply Jennifer's trust of him went. But it did. She'd given him the gift of her body, shared the most intimate act there was between a man and a woman. Why couldn't she trust him with her innermost secrets, as well?

"Jack?" Jennifer said, her clothes bundled up in her arms.

"What? Oh. Yeah, I'm getting it in gear.''

He rolled to his feet and dressed quickly, shrugging into his jacket as he stood by the front door.

"I'll see you later," he said. "I won't come back until I know that Joey's in school so there won't be a hassle about him wanting to stay home and help me with the repairs with his mighty hammer.''

Jennifer nodded. "Fine.''

Jack slid one hand to the nape of Jennifer's neck and kissed her. "Thank you, Jennifer. I mean that sincerely—thank you," he said quietly, then turned and left the house, closing the door behind him with a soft *click*.

"And *I* thank *you*," Jennifer whispered, staring at the door, "for making me feel so special, so womanly, so incredibly alive."

With a wistful sigh and a gentle smile on her lips, Jennifer headed for bed.

The next morning, Jack slid onto a chair at a table in the dining room at Hamilton House. He smiled and greeted Andrea and Brandon, Aunt Charity and Aunt Prudence.

"I'm running a little late," he said. "I slept longer than usual."

"It's probably because of the altitude here in Prescott," Andrea said. "Being a mile high makes many people tired until they adjust to it."

"Yep, that's it, I imagine," Jack said, picking up the menu that had been left for him by the waitress. "The altitude."

"So?" Brandon said. "Report, Jack. Do you have any information to share with us about Jennifer?"

"Yeah, big boy," Aunt Charity said. "What have you learned? Andrea and Brandon filled Pru and me in on your theory that Jennifer was unhappy with Joe Mackane. We all assumed the opposite because she named Joey after his father. We figured Jennifer refused to even date because she was holding fast to memories of sweet bliss with her husband."

"Which is fine to a point," Prudence said, "but there comes a time when a person should move forward with their life… It was distressing enough to us that Jennifer seemed to be living in the past when that past had been, to her, near perfection. To think it might have been just the opposite is heartbreaking. If that's true, we must help her free herself of those memories of misery.''

''I think I'll have pancakes,'' Jack said, signaling to the waitress.

Brandon drummed his fingers impatiently on the tablecloth as Jack placed his order, then sipped the hot coffee the waitress had poured into his cup. ''Come on, MacAllister,'' Brandon said. ''What, if anything, do you have to tell us?''

Jack frowned as he stared into the coffee cup. Damn, he thought, he was suddenly very uncomfortable with the idea of *reporting* on whatever subtle little clues he'd picked up regarding Jennifer's marriage to Mackane.

He now knew Jennifer did not believe that Joe Mackane would have been a devoted and loving father to Joey. He didn't know why she felt that way, only that she did.

He could make this group's day—this committee-to-save-Jennifer-from-herself—by passing along that tidbit. But he was registering a sense of protectiveness and possessiveness about Jennifer, about the special world the two of them created when they were together, a place where no one else was allowed to enter.

Was he being totally selfish? A really rotten guy? If what he divulged to Andrea, Brandon and the aunts made it possible for them to help Jennifer, she could very well embrace the thought of a future with a special man—a husband for her, a father for Joey.

Damn, he hated the idea of some other guy touching Jennifer, holding and kissing her, making love to her in the secret, dark hours of the night. Really, *really* hated that thought.

Ah, hell, he was boggling his mind again. Why was he doing this to himself? He and Jennifer had reached an understanding about the temporary, no-strings-attached status of their relationship. They'd discussed it like mature adults and reached ground rules that were acceptable to both of them.

He should be kicking back and enjoying the time he had left with Jennifer while he was in Prescott. But, oh, no, not him. Now he was *thinking* again, and turning his beleaguered mind into scrambled eggs.

"Pancakes," the waitress said.

Jack jerked in his chair as he was brought back to attention, then moved his coffee cup out of the way so a huge plate could be placed in front of him. He had, he realized, staring at the tower of pancakes, lost his appetite.

"All set?" the waitress said.

"Yes. Fine," Jack said. "Thank you."

"Are you back with us now, buddy?" Brandon said. "You were so deep in thought, I swear they could have dropped a bomb in here, and you wouldn't have noticed."

"Yeah, well..." Jack's voice trailed off, and he busied himself buttering the pancakes and dribbling syrup over them from a small china pitcher.

"There he goes again," Brandon said, throwing up his hands. "Zoned."

Andrea nibbled absently on a piece of toast as she

studied Jack. "There's something troubling you, isn't there, Jack," she said finally.

Jack took a bite of pancakes, chewed, swallowed, then sighed. "Look," he said, sweeping his gaze over everyone at the table. "How would you feel if a group of people were discussing you in a very personal manner behind your back? People you believed were your friends and cared about you very deeply. It's pretty tacky, you know what I mean?"

"But we're doing this because we *do* care about Jennifer," Brandon said. "Hey, you were the one who brought up the possibility that Jennifer had a lousy marriage. This was your plan, MacAllister. Now you're on our case because we agree that we should pursue it because Jennifer is part of our family and we love her. What's with you?"

"Honey, calm down," Andrea said to Brandon. "Jack is obviously having second thoughts about reporting what he may have discovered about Jennifer's past. We have to respect that."

"No, we don't," Brandon said. "How are we going to help Jennifer if we don't know if she needs us to help her?" He frowned. "Did that make sense?"

Aunt Charity narrowed her eyes as she stared at Jack. "Something's cooking in the kitchen. Okay, big boy, what's going on?"

Jack pushed his plate away, unable to take another bite of the sweet, gooey breakfast.

"Nothing is 'going on,' Aunt Charity," he said. "I just... Ah, hell, forget it. Can we just cancel this whole plan? Forget I ever brought up the subject of Jennifer's past, her marriage to Mackane?"

"No," Brandon and Aunt Charity said in unison.

"I'm a tad confused, Jack dear," Aunt Prudence said. "Our hearts are in the right place on this matter, as I believe you know. Don't you feel that Jennifer is worth whatever efforts we might make on her behalf?"

"Is Jennifer worth—" Jack began. "Aunt Prudence, Jennifer is one in a million—a very rare, special and wonderful woman. She's real, honest, open and is a terrific mother to a fantastic little boy who…" He glanced at Andrea, who was smiling at him. "What's *your* problem?" he said gruffly.

"*I* don't have one," Andrea said. "*I'm* not the person at this table who is acting like a protective knight of the Round Table, or whatever, in regard to Jennifer. Nope, not me."

"Give it a rest," Jack said gruffly. "I just don't think it's appropriate to analyze every little thing a person does or says, when they have no clue you're doing it."

"It's based on love, dear," Aunt Prudence said.

Jack stared up at the ceiling for what felt like a long moment, then shook his head as he looked at the group again. "Okay," he said wearily. "I'm outnumbered. I give up. Jennifer let it slip that she didn't believe Joe Mackane would have been a loving and devoted father to Joey."

"Oh, my stars," Aunt Prudence said. "How very distressing."

"A dud as a daddy, huh?" Aunt Charity said. "What about as a husband? Get a scoop on that?"

"No," Jack said, getting to his feet. He dug into

the pocket of his jeans, then dropped several bills onto the table. "I have things to do. See ya."

He turned and strode across the dining room.

Jack walked along the sidewalk, mentally grumbling as he headed for Jennifer's house. He shouldn't have told Andrea, Brandon and the aunts what Jennifer had said about Mackane not being good father material for Joey, he admonished himself. That was Jennifer's private business, and not for public knowledge.

Then again, the public, in the form of the four people at the table at Hamilton House, weren't nosy nobodies. They loved Jennifer, wanted only the best for her.

If Jennifer had, indeed, had a miserable marriage with Joe Mackane, it would be those same four caring people who just might be able to help her let go of the painful memories and move forward.

Who was *he* to be spilling the beans regarding Jennifer and Joe? *Jennifer and Joe.* Erase that. He didn't like the sound of their names as a couple echoing in his mind. *Jennifer and Joe. Joe and Jennifer.* No. No way.

Forget it.

It was supposed to be Jennifer and *Jack.*

Jack nearly stumbled at the impact of his last rambling thought. Where in the hell had that come from? The way it had flowed in his head made it seem as though *Jack* was next in line for being the groom guy, the daddy bear.

Not a chance.

Slow down, MacAllister, he ordered himself. He

was being too hard on himself. Of course he'd think in terms of Jennifer and Jack because, for now, they were together, and would be until he left Prescott to begin his new life in California.

So there was nothing wrong with mentally linking his name with Jennifer's for the time being. They were, after all, engaged in an affair.

Jack frowned and shoved his hands into his jacket pockets as he trudged on. *Affair,* his mind echoed. That was a rather pitiful word to describe what he was sharing with Jennifer. Affairs were centered on sex, on physical gratification, with no emotional involvement.

No, he wasn't having an *affair* with Jennifer Mackane. It was more than that—richer, deeper, meaningful. They hadn't engaged in sex, they'd made love.

And there *were* emotions involved. He cared for Jennifer, respected her. It mattered—hell, yes, it mattered—that he never did anything to hurt Jennifer, never made her cry.

Fine. That was fine. There were no dangerous emotions lurking in the shadows, threatening to sneak up on him, to cause him to wake up one morning and discover that he'd committed the ultimate act of stupidity and fallen head-over-heels in love with Jennifer.

Nope. Couldn't happen. He and Jennifer knew where they stood in regard to their...their relationship. Everything was under control.

Jennifer's house came into view, and Jack quickened his step, aware of a sense of anticipation over seeing Jennifer, kissing her, hearing her laughter.

As for the I Spy number he was engaged in for Andrea, Brandon and the aunts...well, he'd figure that out later, decide what was the right thing to do.

Yeah, he'd tackle that problem later, because right now he was within minutes of holding Jennifer Mackane in his arms.

Chapter Nine

On Saturday morning, Jennifer lay in bed blissfully indulging herself by reliving the events that had taken place since she and Jack had first made love on Tuesday night.

So-o-o wonderful, she thought dreamily. The lovemaking she and Jack had shared every night since then had been incredibly beautiful, like nothing she'd experienced before or even imagined possible in her most fantasy-filled daydreams.

But that intimacy was only a part of what had made these days and nights so special, so meaningful. She'd been warmed to the very tips of her toes as she'd watched Joey and Jack working together on the repairs of the house.

Jack was so patient with Joey—answered her son's endless questions, allowed Joey to take an active part in the project, which undoubtedly was slowing Jack down.

There was lunch together, too, the three of them sitting at the kitchen table, chatting and laughing as they consumed the meal she had prepared.

Joey now wanted his sandwich cut just like Jack's, the same number of ice cubes in his glass as Jack had in his, and carefully spread his napkin over one knee precisely the way Jack did.

Joey hung on Jack's every word, had reversed his recent stand that bubbles in his bath were for babies when Jack declared bubble baths to be a majorly fun event.

Jennifer frowned and shifted restlessly on the bed.

Was Joey becoming too attached to Jack? Was her little boy headed for heartbreak whenever Jack left, even though he was reminded, when the opportunity presented itself, that Jack was leaving for California before Christmas?

Was Joey listening to what was said to him, but refusing to really *hear* that Jack would be walking out of their lives forever in just a few weeks?

Forever, Jennifer's mind echoed. Jack would be gone...forever.

A chill swept through her and she pulled the blankets to beneath her chin.

Jennifer, don't, she ordered herself. She knew Jack was leaving, knew that what they were now sharing was temporary. She *knew* that.

Jack's definite departure was, in fact, the reason she'd had enough courage to enter into a relationship with him in the first place. There was no danger of Jack asking more of her than she was prepared to give, because he wouldn't be there to pressure her.

She knew all that.

Then why did the image of Jack saying goodbye for the last time cause such a cold emptiness to suddenly consume her? The future—the days, weeks, months, years—loomed before her with such a bleak sameness, as if something of vital importance was definitely missing.

Oh, dear heaven, what was happening to her? Was she, not Joey, the one whose heart would be shattered when Jack said his final farewell?

"No, no, no," she said, flinging back the blankets and sitting up on the edge of the bed. "Don't be ridiculous. I'm fine. In control. Know the facts. I'm hunky-dory. A-okay."

"Who are you talking to, Mom?" Joey said, coming into the bedroom.

Jennifer shoved her feet into her slippers. "Big Bird. I talk to my slippers when you're not around to listen to me. Big Bird is a great audience." She smiled at her son. "How's my big boy this morning? Ready for some breakfast, my sweet?"

Joey crawled up onto the bed and lay down. "I'm not hungry," he said. "My stomach hurts on my belly button."

Jennifer frowned and turned to place her hand on Joey's forehead. "You're a little warm," she said. "Why don't you snuggle in there and see if you can go back to sleep for a bit? I'll bring you some juice, then you try to snore. Okay?"

"No, Mom, I want to help Jack when he comes," Joey whined.

"Jack won't be here for a while. It's very early, you know. I imagine he's still snoozing away in his bed in Uncle Brandon's hotel. You have plenty of time to get some more rest."

"But I'm his partner, Mom," Joey said, his eyes filling with tears. "We do men stuff together fixing up the house. What if I'm asleep when he comes? Jack needs me to hand him nails and everything. He really does. I want to be with Jack, Mommy."

"Shh, sweetie, don't get upset," Jennifer said, tucking the blankets around him. "I'll wake you up when Jack arrives."

"Promise?" Joey said, then sniffled.

"I promise."

"'Kay."

"Stay awake long enough to drink some juice, and I need to take your temperature, too. I'll be right back."

"'Kay."

An hour later, Jennifer was dressed in jeans and a white fisherman's-knit sweater. She sat on the edge of her bed, watching Joey sleep. His cheeks were flushed and his slumber was restless.

Should she call Ben? she wondered. Joey's Uncle Ben Rizzoli was Joey's doctor, and she knew he wouldn't mind if she disturbed him at home on a Saturday morning.

Well, maybe Ben wouldn't welcome the intrusion of a ringing telephone, considering that he and Megan were on their honeymoon, for all practical purposes.

The couple was planning on an official wedding

trip in the spring, but they *were* newly married and— No, she'd see how Joey was feeling when he woke up, and bother Ben only if it was absolutely necessary.

Jennifer smoothed the blankets over Joey, brushed his moist hair from his forehead, then after one last lingering look at him, wandered out of the bedroom and down the hallway.

In the living room she opened the drapes on the front windows. As she now did every morning when she performed the ritual, her gaze zeroed in immediately on the spot on the sidewalk where she had first seen Jack MacAllister staring at her house.

The remembrance of that morning always brought a sense of joy with it, along with a flash of embarrassment as she mentally relived her performance in the dining room at Hamilton House when Jack made his "stalking" appearance that evening.

"I'm Jack MacAllister. Not Jack the Ripper," she said in a deep voice, then laughed. "Oh, I was such an idiot. What a show I put on."

Her glance was drawn once again to the spot on the sidewalk where Jack had stood on that life-changing morning. Her smile faded as she stared at it, suddenly acutely aware that the space was empty. Jack wasn't there, and in a handful of weeks would never be there again.

Jack would be gone, taking with him the warmth of his smile, his compelling chocolate fudge sauce eyes, the rich timbre of his voice and chuckle, the strength and gentleness of his arms, his magnificent body that carried her away to glorious heights of ecstasy when they made love.

"He isn't mine to keep," Jennifer whispered. "Like Joey says, I have to give him back."

Jennifer lifted her chin and ignored the sting of tears in her eyes.

Fine. That was how it should be. If Jack had moved to Prescott, instead of just being a temporary visitor, she never would have engaged in any kind of relationship with him at all.

That would have been too risky, far too emotionally dangerous. She might very well have fallen in love with him over time, lost her heart to him, which was something she'd vowed she'd never *ever* do with any man again.

And Jack might have fallen in love with her, then pushed her to make a commitment to forever—even asked her to marry him, for heaven's sake. She would have been forced to break off her relationship with him, ending what they had in heartache and, possibly, anger.

Jennifer looked at the empty sidewalk and nodded.

So be it. This was how it should be—the only way it could be. Yes, she'd miss Jack for a while when he left, but that was to be expected. She'd have her lovely memories to hold her in good stead in the months and years ahead.

"Mommy!" Joey yelled, jerking Jennifer from her thoughts.

She turned and ran across the room and down the hall to her bedroom. "I'm here, sweetie," she said, coming to a teetering halt by her bed.

"My tummy is jiggly," Joey said.

"Oops." Jennifer scooped Joey into her arms.

"We know what that means. You're going to give back that juice you drank."

After Joey had redistributed the juice, Jennifer washed his face, then settled him once again in her bed. "Does your belly button still hurt?" she said, sitting down next to him.

"My whole stomach hurts really bad," Joey said, then burst into tears. "It hurts worse than anything in the whole wide world."

"Well, it's time for me to call Uncle Ben and ask him what we should do about that tummy, Joey."

"Tell Uncle Ben to fix it 'cause I gotta help Jack, Mommy."

"I will. I'll tell him." She kissed Joey on the forehead, then got to her feet. "I'll be back as soon as I've spoken with Uncle Ben."

"'Kay. Oh-h-h, it hurts," Joey said, thrashing on the bed.

A cold fist of fear tightened within Jennifer, and she turned and ran from the room. As she entered the living room, a knock sounded at the front door.

"Jack," she whispered, coming to a halt.

She hurried to the door and flung it open.

"Good morning, lovely lady," Jack said, smiling. "I'm reporting for duty to—"

Jennifer grabbed Jack's arm and dragged him into the house, slamming the door closed behind him. "Joey's sick," she said. "I have to call Ben."

"You're pale as a ghost," Jack said, frowning. "How sick is Joey?" He shrugged out of his jacket and tossed it onto the back of the sofa. "What's wrong with him?"

"He has a really terrible stomachache," she said,

her voice trembling. "I've never seen him in this kind of pain, Jack."

"Okay," Jack said. "Go call Ben. Where's Joey?"

"In my bed."

"I'll stay with him while you call. Go."

"Thank you. Thank you, Jack."

As Jack headed across the room, Jennifer went into the kitchen and looked at a sheet of paper tacked to the wall above the telephone. She lifted the receiver and punched in the number.

"Be there, Ben," she said as she heard the phone at the other end ringing. "Please be home."

"Hello?"

"Oh, Ben, thank goodness," Jennifer said, pressing one hand to her forehead. "This is Jennifer. Joey has a terrible pain in his stomach, and I—"

"Whoa," Ben said. "Slow down. Take a deep breath and get a grip. I need to ask you some questions."

"Yes. Okay. I'm calm."

"Good. Jennifer, did Joey say where the pain was in his stomach?"

"Where? Well, at first he said his belly button hurt, but now it's his whole stomach. He has a fever and he upchucked and—"

"Halt. This is important. Did Joey have the pain first, before he became nauseated?"

"Yes," Jennifer said, nodding.

"Oh, boy. It's textbook classic."

"Textbook classic what? What's wrong with him?"

"Didn't you have your appendix out when we

were kids? I seem to remember playing checkers with you while you were recuperating."

"Yes, I was ten."

"Did Joey's father have his removed?"

"Oh, I don't know, Ben, I— No, wait, yes, he did. He said that he was in high school and couldn't play football for several weeks."

"That cooks it," Ben said. "The genetic factor plays a heavy role in appendicitis."

"Dear heaven."

"Look, I'll meet you in the emergency room at the hospital, rather than at my office. That will save a lot of time."

"Are you going to operate on Joey? Take out his appendix?" Jennifer said, nearly shrieking. "He's just a baby, Ben."

"No, he's not. He's a strong, healthy boy who has all the classic symptoms of a hot appendix. I'll know for sure when I examine him. I'm not a surgeon, you know, Jennifer, but I'll be with him every minute if it comes to that. Do not—do *not*—give Joey any more to eat or drink. Got that?"

"Yes. I hear you."

"Wrap Joey up and bring him in. I'll meet you at the hospital. Drive carefully, Jennifer. Keep your cool. I realize that you're facing this alone, but—"

"No, no, Jack is here."

"Jack? Oh, Jack MacAllister? That friend of Brandon's? I met him the other day. Nice guy. Well, good, you're *not* alone. You and Jack can do this together. See you in a few minutes. 'Bye."

"'Bye."

Jennifer hung up the receiver, drew a shuddering breath, then ran from the room.

Jennifer paced restlessly around the waiting room in the hospital, glancing often at her watch, then the clock on the wall.

Jack entered the small, nicely furnished area, carrying two foam cups.

"Coffee," he said. "Come and sit down, Jennifer, and drink this. Okay?"

"No, thank you, Jack. I'm stressed enough without getting the jitters from too much coffee." She shook her head. "I can't believe this is happening. Joey was fine yesterday, and now he's in surgery having his appendix removed. He was so frightened by the pain and by all that took place after we arrived here. I felt so helpless. I still do."

Jack set the cups on one of the tables, then closed the distance between them. He pulled her close, and she wrapped her arms around his waist as she laid her head on his chest.

"I'm not handling this very well," she said. "Joey has always been so healthy, has never had anything beyond an occasional cold or bout of the flu. And now? He's being operated on, for God's sake, and I'm falling apart."

"Hey," Jack said, rubbing her back gently, "don't be so hard on yourself. This is a scary deal. I would have done anything to stop the pain Joey was in as we drove over here. I felt powerless. It didn't matter how big and strong a man I might be— my size and strength were worthless."

"Then you *do* understand how I feel."

"Damn straight, I do," Jack said. "Joey and I are supposed to be pounding nails together right now, having a great old time. I hate what he's going through, Jennifer. I really hate it."

He paused. "But, hey, everything will be fine. Ben is a top-notch doctor, and he personally chose the surgeon for Joey. Everything is under control." He chuckled. "Except us. We're coming unglued."

"Ah, the joys of parenthood," Jennifer said, smiling. "You don't know what will happen from one minute to the next." She lifted her head to meet Jack's gaze. "You were wonderful with Joey during the drive over here. You were so calm, talked to him, got him to relax at least as much as he could, considering the pain he was in. I do believe that you're a natural-born father."

Alarm bells went off in Jack's head and he stiffened slightly as he looked at Jennifer. What was this? he thought. A little push, a hint at what might very well be Jennifer's hidden agenda?

Had she changed her previous mindset about never remarrying?

Was she zeroing in on him to be her next husband and a father for Joey?

Had she shifted gears on him, and he'd been too dumb to realize it?

Damn it, was Jennifer Mackane like all the other women he'd been involved with? Was she now hell-bent on getting what *she* wanted from him?

"Yeah, well," he said, no hint of a smile on his face. "I operate with kids under the same guidelines that Joey does with his uncles. I give them back."

"Mmm," Jennifer said, frowning. "Joey certainly isn't very happy with that premise these days.''

''Well, I'm very satisfied with mine regarding children. When I move to California, there will be MacAllister kids coming out of the woodwork. I'll borrow a few when the mood strikes, then return them when I've had enough and they're driving me nuts.''

''Has Joey been a pest while you've been working together on the house?''

''Hey, no way,'' Jack said. ''Not for a second. I've enjoyed spending time with him.''

''Doing 'men' stuff,'' Jennifer said, smiling again.

''Yep. However, I must admit that the *man* stuff I do with you when we're alone is much more to my liking.''

''Hush,'' Jennifer said, feeling a flush of heat stain her cheeks. ''We're in a busy hospital, and someone might hear you.'' She sighed and eased out of Jack's arms. ''Back to reality. We're in a hospital and my son is being operated on. What's taking so long?''

Jennifer began to wander around the room again, her troubled gaze alternating among the clock on the wall, her watch and the doorway.

Jack slouched into a chair and studied her. He wished he could peer into Jennifer's brain, find out what she was really thinking. Man, he hated having these sudden doubts about Jennifer, hated even entertaining the idea that she might not be who she presented herself to be.

Maybe her words had just been an idle remark, a

compliment. She thought he was a natural-born father and had told him so. End of story. No big deal.

Or was it?

Jack took a deep breath and let it out slowly, puff-
ing his cheeks. Enough of this. For now, he'd just
concentrate on waiting for word of how Joey was.
That was plenty on his plate at the moment.

Besides, he reasoned, so what if Jennifer had
taken a fresh look at her future and decided that,
yes, sir, Jack MacAllister would do a dandy job as
a husband for her and a father for Joey? It didn't
mean squat if she'd changed her views on the subject of commitment because in a few weeks he'd be
long gone, anyway.

Ah, hell, who was he kidding? It *did* matter. He
wanted, *needed* Jennifer to be as real and honest as
he believed her to be.

Just once in his life, he would like to be able to
savor memories of time shared with a woman, not
look back with anger and self-disgust at his own
gullibility.

No, it was even more than that. He wanted and
needed to be able to cherish his memories of Jennifer Mackane.

"I should have asked Ben how long this would
take," Jennifer said, interrupting Jack's racing
thoughts. "Oh, darn, why didn't I? Maybe a nurse
would know. Yes. I'll go ask a nurse."

"You're going to be very upset if you're not in
this room when Ben comes," Jack said quietly.

Jennifer sighed and sat down on a sofa. "Yes,
you're right."

"Always."

Jennifer laughed. "Is that a fact?"

"Guaranteed."

"Oh, Jack, thank you," she said, smiling at him warmly. "You've been fantastic through all of this. I'd be out of my mind if I was caged up in this room alone."

"You have a lot of friends in Prescott," he said. "You could have called someone to come over here and wait with you."

"I suppose. But I probably wouldn't have. I'm set on automatic independence." She paused. "When I was speaking with Ben on the telephone at the house, he said something to me that keeps popping into my head."

"Oh? What?"

"I told Ben that you were there with me, and he said it was good that I wasn't alone. 'You and Jack can do this together,' he said."

Jack straightened in the chair and narrowed his eyes as he looked at Jennifer. "What point are you trying to make here?" he said, a slight edge to his voice.

Jennifer shrugged. "Only that I might have fallen into a pattern of behavior of being *too* independent, of not allowing myself to ask for help, to lean a little, to seek comfort from time to time from those who care about me. I'll have to give that some very serious thought when things calm down again."

"You do that," Jack said, lunging to his feet and glaring down at her. "Who knows, Jennifer? You might decide to swoop up that bridal bouquet you caught and go find yourself a groom guy, a daddy bear. How does that strike you, Ms. Mackane?"

"For heaven's sake, Jack," she said, frowning in confusion. "Where did all that nonsense come from? And why do you seem so angry all of a sudden?"

"I..." Jack stopped speaking, closed his eyes for a moment, and shook his head before looking at Jennifer again. "I'm sorry. Forget I said that. This waiting is hard on the nerves, and I'm stressed. Just erase that last bit I barked at you. Okay? Can you do that?"

"I...I guess so," Jennifer said, getting to her feet. "But you made me sound like a woman on a husband hunt, or some such thing. My goodness, Jack, don't you know me better than that by now? How could you even imply that I— Oh!"

Jennifer gasped as Jack closed the short distance between then, gripped her upper arms...and kissed her.

But...she thought hazily. She needed to understand why Jack had said such nasty things to her with a strange and bitter edge to his voice that she'd never heard from him before. She...really needed...to understand because... Oh, never mind.

Don't think, Jennifer, Jack mentally pleaded. *Don't dwell on the rotten junk I said to you. Just feel. Just feel. Don't think.*

"I hate to interrupt, but..." Ben said with a chuckle as he entered the room.

Jennifer and Jack jumped apart, then spun around to face Ben.

"Joey?" Jennifer said, clasping her hands tightly beneath her chin.

Ben looked at Jennifer, then Jack, then back at

Jennifer, then chuckled again. "I'll be damned," he said, grinning.

"Ben!" Jennifer yelled. "Joey?"

"He's fine, fine, fine," Ben said. "Came through like a champ. His appendix definitely needed to get out of there, but we got it in plenty of time. We'll keep him here for two, maybe three, days, depending on how he does. He'll have to take it easy for a couple of weeks. I'd keep him home from kindergarten, if I were you, to be assured he doesn't run, jump—well, be an active little boy. Okay?"

"Yes, I understand. May I see him now, Ben?" Jennifer said.

"Mosey on over to the pediatric wing," Ben said. "Joey will be in his room in about half an hour."

Jennifer kissed Ben on the cheek, then Jack shook the doctor's hand. "Thank you," Jennifer and Jack said in unison.

"You're welcome. I'll see you later." Ben crossed the room and stopped at the doorway. "Go back to doing what you were when I interrupted. I'd write a prescription for that jazz if I could. It cures a lot of ills. 'Bye."

"'Bye," Jennifer said, then added to Jack, "So much for keeping our relationship a secret." She paused. "Well, so be it. The important thing is that Joey is all right. Let's go to the children's wing and wait for him in his room. Okay?"

"Absolutely," Jack said, pulling her close. "But first, I believe that people should always follow doctor's orders."

"Do tell," Jennifer said, smiling.

"I show much better than I tell," he said, lowering his head toward hers.

"Prove it."

"I will."

And he did.

Chapter Ten

Joey Mackane was *not* a happy patient.

He had a nagging headache from the anesthesia, his tummy hurt, he did not like the intravenous needle that had been inserted and taped into place on the back of his hand, nor the bars on the sides of his bed that made him feel, he whined, like a "dumb baby." The hospital smelled funny, and he wanted to go home. *Now.*

It was a very long, exhausting day.

Jennifer selected several books from the cart a candy striper produced, but Joey pouted and complained through the reading of each one that he'd heard that story before and it was dumb, dumb, dumb.

Jack went to the hospital gift shop and returned with a coloring book and crayons, but Joey rejected the offering, stating that his crayon box at home had a sharpener attached. Crayon boxes without sharpeners were really dumb.

In the early evening, the surgeon and Ben paid a visit and the I.V. was removed from Joey's hand.

After the doctors had gone, a nurse arrived with a dish of green Jell-O. She swung the table over in front of Joey and placed the dish and a spoon in front of him. "Enjoy," she said, smiling, then left the room.

"I hate dumb green Jell-O," Joey said, flinging one hand through the air. The dish went flying, splashing green jelly over the blanket on the bed.

"Oh, Joey," Jennifer said, getting to her feet from the chair next to the bed. "That wasn't a nice thing to do. We'll have to get a different blanket now and— Please, sweetheart, calm down. Okay?"

"No, no, no," Joey yelled. "I hate this place. I hate green Jell-O. I hate you, too, Mom, 'cause you won't take me home right now. I hate you. I hate you."

It was too much, it really was. The worry, the stress, the seemingly endless hours attempting to make Joey happy caught up with Jennifer in an emotional rush. She spun around as tears filled her eyes, and pressed trembling fingertips to her lips.

"That's it," Jack said. He rose from the chair he'd been slouched in across the room and strode to the bed, moving past Jennifer to bend over and look directly into Joey's eyes.

"Listen up, my friend," he said sternly. "I've sat in this room all day while you've whined and fussed, and I've had enough. I know what you've been through isn't fun, but you're going to be fine. There are kids in this hospital who are very, very sick, Joey, but you aren't one of them. You'll be as good as new in time to celebrate Thanksgiving.

"I thought you were my pal, my partner," he continued. "What happened to the big boy who has been helping repair things at the house all week? All I can see is a kid who is whining like a baby."

Jennifer turned around. "Jack, don't. Joey is—"

"Joey is going to shape up right now," Jack went on, still looking at the little boy. "Aren't you, sport? You're also going to apologize to your mother for saying that you hate her. Are you my buddy, or not?" He extended his hand toward Joey. "Make up your mind."

Joey looked at Jack's hand, at his face, then back at his hand. He lifted his own little hand and placed it in Jack's big one. "I still want to be your buddy, Jack," Joey said quietly.

Jack wrapped his fingers around Joey's hand. "And?" Jack said. "What do you have to say to your mother?"

"I'm sorry, Mommy," Joey said. "I don't hate you. I love you more than the whole wide world. I hate green Jell-O, but that's okay, 'cause you didn't cook it for me. I won't act like a baby brat anymore. I promise."

"Oh, Joey," Jennifer said, sniffling. "I love you, too, so much. I know this has all been very frightening for you and—"

"Actually," Jack interrupted, releasing Joey's hand, "it's very cool, sport. You get to eat in bed and watch television, and you don't have to do your chores while you're here. I'm going to ship you out and crawl in that bed myself.''

Joey laughed. "You can't do that, Jack. This is *my* bed. Can I do the remote control for the TV?''

Jack picked up the remote from the side table and handed it to Joey. "Go for it," Jack said. "You can channel surf until they tell you it's time to go to sleep. I'm taking your mom home now because she's really tired.''

"'Kay." Joey's attention was riveted on the television mounted on a platform high on the far wall. He whizzed through the channels. "Zoom. Zoom.''

"Jack," Jennifer said, glaring at him, "I'm staying with Joey until he falls asleep.''

"No, you are not," Jack said, folding his arms over his chest. "Have you looked in the mirror lately? You're pale, have dark smudges beneath your eyes and—Jennifer, you're dead on your feet. Kiss Joey good-night, then I'm taking you home.''

Jennifer narrowed her eyes and planted her hands on her hips. "How dare you try to take control of my life, my decisions, my—my person, like some kind of dictator on a macho trip?" she said none too quietly. "You have no right to—''

"Mom," Joey said, "could you yell at Jack kinda quieter, please? I can't hear the TV.''

"Yeah," Jack said, grinning at Jennifer. "Yell at me kinda quieter. You *are* in a hospital, you know. There are rules about quieter yelling.''

"Oh, good grief," Jennifer said, dropping her face into her hands. "I don't believe this.''

"Zoom. Zoom," Joey said, still zipping through the channels on the television.

Jack eased Jennifer's hands from her face with a gentle touch, and she lifted her head slowly to meet his gaze.

"I'm not attempting to control your life, Jennifer," he said quietly. "I'm taking a stand here because I care about you. I'm trying to do what's best for you as I see it."

He paused. "And for Joey, too. If someone didn't pull the plug on his behavior, he would have kept it up and been completely convinced that he was miserable. This isn't a macho trip, it's a caring trip. Okay?"

Fresh tears filled Jennifer's eyes and she sighed. "'Kay."

"Good," Jack said. "Kiss Joey good-night."

Jennifer did as instructed, then Jack and Joey exchanged a high five.

"I'll call Grandma and Grandpa in Phoenix," Jennifer said to her son, "and tell them what happened and what a brave, big boy you are."

"Don't tell them 'bout the baby bratty part," Joey said, frowning.

"No, I won't sweetheart. Good night."

"'Night, Mom. 'Night, Jack."

"See you tomorrow, buddy," Jack said.

"Zoom. Zoom," Joey said, his attention once again on the television.

In Jennifer's living room, Jack stood just inside the closed front door, but didn't remove his jacket when Jennifer tossed her coat over the back of the sofa.

"I take it that you're still mad as hell at me,"

Jack said. "You haven't said even one word since we left Joey's room."

Jennifer sank onto the sofa, leaned her head back and stared at the ceiling. "I don't know what I'm feeling," she said softly. "Mad as hell at you for taking control of the situation? Experiencing warm fuzzies for your caring enough to do it? I just don't know. It's all very confusing, and I'm much too tired to even attempt to figure it out."

"Would you like me to go so you can get some rest?" Jack asked, remaining by the door.

Jennifer got to her feet slowly, then turned and looked at Jack. "What if I don't know the answer to that, either?" she said.

"We flip a coin?" he said, smiling. Then his smile faded and he shoved his hands into his jacket pockets. "I don't want to leave you tonight, Jennifer, if my vote counts for anything. It's been a long, grueling, pretty frightening day, but...well, we did it, we got through it...together. I want to finish this day with you, hold you until you fall asleep, know for certain that you're getting the rest you need. I'm not pushing for making love—I just want to hold you close, be with you. Be here *for* you."

And she, Jennifer thought, with a flash of panic, she was... Oh, God, slowly but surely falling in love with Jack MacAllister. He was chipping away, piece by emotional piece, at her protective wall, crumbling it into dust.

No, no, no, this mustn't happen. She'd promised herself, vowed, she'd never love again, never trust a man enough again to lose her heart to him.

To fall deeply in love with Jack MacAllister...if

she hadn't already...oh, she didn't want to know the true depths of her blossoming love for him. Jack was guaranteed heartbreak because he was walking out of her life in a handful of weeks. To be gone forever.

She had to send him away. *Now. Right now.* She had to rebuild her wall quickly, quickly, and ignore whatever messages her heart might be whispering. She had to protect herself from Jack and—heaven help her—from herself.

"Jennifer?" Jack said. "Talk to me. Do you want me to leave?"

Yes! her mind screamed.

"No," she heard herself say, an echo of tears in her voice. "No, I don't want to...to be alone."

Jack nodded, then began to unbutton his jacket while still looking directly at Jennifer. Quicksand, he thought suddenly. He was being pulled deeper and deeper into Jennifer's life, her world.

Emotional quicksand, that was what it was, and he wasn't doing one damn thing to free himself.

He was, in fact, doing exactly the opposite. He'd felt the knot in his gut dissolve when Jennifer had said she wanted him to stay. He'd made his heartfelt statement, then waited with a sense of dread that she'd send him away to spend a lonely night at Hamilton House.

What was he doing? He'd experienced flashes of doubt regarding Jennifer's true agenda, wondering if he'd once again misjudged a woman and was being played for a fool.

But in between? Hell, he was scrambling for the right words to express his honest caring, his sincere desire to stand by her side during this crisis with Joey.

Zoom, he thought dryly. His brain was doing what Joey was with the television remote. Zooming around with no rhyme or reason, making no sense, driving him crazy.

"I need to call my parents," Jennifer said, bringing Jack back to attention.

Jack shrugged out of his jacket and set it next to Jennifer's coat on the back of the sofa. "Okay," he said. "Do you want me to start a fire in the hearth, or would you prefer to go right to bed and get some rest?"

"I'm too wired to sleep. A fire would be nice." Jennifer paused. "Are you hungry? Those sandwiches you brought us from the hospital cafeteria weren't great. I could fix us some—"

"No," he said. "I'm fine. Don't worry about me, Jennifer. We're concentrating on you tonight, and that doesn't include your cooking anything."

"This is *my* night?" she said, smiling slightly. "Like I won the lottery or something?"

"Or something," he said, chuckling. "Go call your folks, but leave out the part about Joey acting rotten. You promised him you wouldn't blow the whistle on him."

Jennifer cocked her head to one side and studied Jack intently.

"What?" he said finally.

"How did you know that the time had come to get firm with Joey? I'm his mother, and I was practically standing on my head in an attempt to please him, make him happy, and failing miserably. You just knew what needed to be done. How? Why?''

Jack shrugged and walked to the fireplace. He hunkered down in front of it, opened the screen and began to place kindling on the grate.

''You are *definitely* a natural-born father,'' Jennifer said, starting across the room. ''I'll go telephone my parents.''

Jack's head snapped around and he watched Jennifer disappear from view. He looked at the grate again, then threw some kindling onto it with more force than was necessary.

There it was again, he thought, that zinger of Jennifer's that he was a natural-born father, only this time she'd added an emphatic *definitely*. Damn it, where was she going with that nonsense? What foundation was she putting in place?

Ah, MacAllister, give it a rest, Jack told himself, setting a log on the kindling. He'd had a long day, too, and had been scared to death during that drive to the hospital with a crying Joey.

The wait during the surgery hadn't been a picnic, either. He was beat, and had no business now attempting to get a handle on what Jennifer might be after. He wasn't going to think about it any more tonight. Not tonight.

Jack struck a match, started the fire, then closed the screen. He moved backward to lean against the sofa, knees bent, his wrists dangling over them. He stared into the now leaping flames and began to feel himself relax, his muscles loosen.

That Joey was something, he thought, smiling. He'd had Jennifer jumping through hoops for hours on end at the hospital. Any kid would continue to push buttons on a parent that he hadn't been allowed to push before.

Well, he'd called a halt to Joey's performance. Enough had been enough. Joey had seemed almost relieved to be told to knock it off, had been more than ready to be his usual, smiling self. *Zoom. Zoom.* Give a kid a remote control and all was right in the world of being five years old.

How *had* he known that it was time to pull the plug on Joey's act? How had he, bachelor *extraordinaire,* sensed that a firm stand was needed to get Joey squared away?

Jack frowned. Well, hell, maybe he *was* a natural-born father. A father. That was a role he never intended to have because it would include getting married, being a husband, actually believing he'd chosen the right woman to be his life's partner.

Nope. No way. Not with his track record of misjudging the honesty, the *realness,* of every woman he'd ever been in a relationship with. He was a complete dud when it came to being able to see the true colors of members of the female species.

Including Jennifer Mackane?

Don't go there, he ordered himself. Not tonight. He wasn't diving into that muddled part of his brain when he was weary to the bone. He was just going to sit here and enjoy the fire. Enjoy being with Jennifer. Be here for her after her long, exhausting day.

"What a lovely fire," Jennifer said, coming back into the room. "Would you like some brandy?"

Jack accepted the small snifter that Jennifer was

offering him, then she sat down next to him on the floor, holding a snifter of her own.

"When I talked to my dad," she said, "he reminded me that he'd left a bottle of brandy on the top shelf of one of the kitchen cupboards. He said it sounded like it was time to open it and relax after the day I'd had."

"Smart man." Jack lifted his snifter. "Cheers, and all that good stuff."

Jennifer clinked her glass against Jack's, then they each took a sip of the amber liquid.

"Nice," Jack said, nodding. "Very smooth."

"Goodness," Jennifer said, then coughed. "This is potent. One little sip warmed me all the way down to my toes." She laughed. "My mother asked me if Joey was being a good patient. I did a couple of 'Well, um… Well, sort of…' and my mom fell apart laughing."

"Why?"

"She said I might have been ten when I had my appendix out, but I acted about three years old. I fussed, fumed, and—to quote—was an Olympic-form brat. That went on until my father told me that babies went to bed very, very early and that could be arranged for me when I got home from the hospital. I turned into little Miss Sunshine in the next instant."

Jack chuckled. "So, Joey inherited that gene from you, huh?"

"I'm afraid so," she said, smiling. "My father put an end to my pitch-a-fit, just like you did with Joey. You fellas sure are wise."

"Right," Jack said, an edge to his voice. He took

a deep swallow of the brandy. "Natural-born fathers."

Jennifer looked at Jack and frowned. "You sound angry all of a sudden, Jack. Did I miss something here?"

Jack sighed. "No, forget it. I'm just tired." He extended one arm toward Jennifer. "Come here."

She scooted close to him, and he caressed her arm as she rested her head on his shoulder. They finished the rich brandy in silence, then Jack set the snifters on the floor next to him. They still didn't speak as they stared into the flames, allowing themselves to be semi-hypnotized—not thinking, just relaxing.

"Mmm," Jennifer said finally. "This is much better. I think I may live, after all. What a grueling day."

"Yep."

"Thank you for everything, Jack. I can't begin to express—"

"Then don't try," he interrupted, "because it isn't necessary." He kissed her on the forehead. "I was where I wanted to be today. I'm where I want to be tonight. Enough said."

"Okay."

This is *my* night, Jennifer thought, suddenly recalling her earlier conversation with Jack. Well, she wasn't going to spend it beating herself up for having lost her heart to Jack MacAllister. Nor would she use these hours to determine just how deeply she was in love with him.

That she was going to cry in the lonely, dark hours of the night when Jack was gone was now a given. But how badly shattered her heart would be was something she didn't have the energy to deal with now.

No, this was *her* night to do with as she wished, to put her wants and needs absolutely, positively first.

And she wanted to make love with Jack.

Jennifer lifted her head from Jack's shoulder and turned to look at him. "Jack?" she said softly.

He met her gaze. "Hmm?"

She placed one hand on his cheek, then raised up enough to capture his lips with hers. Jack jerked in surprise, then slid one hand to the nape of her neck and returned the kiss with equal intensity.

Heat rocketed through him and his desire soared instantly. He had to force himself to break the kiss, then drew a ragged breath.

"Jennifer," he said, his voice rough, "don't. You're exhausted. Let's not start something here that can't be finished."

"But you said it was my night," she said. "Mine. This is what I choose to do with it. I want you, Jack." She paused. "Of course, if *you're* too tired, then—"

Jennifer's words were smothered by Jack's mouth covering hers in a melting kiss that stole the very breath from her body. She wrapped her arms around his neck, sinking her fingertips into the lush thickness of his hair, urging his mouth harder onto hers.

She was filled with immeasurable joy—a sense of completeness—that was accompanied by raging passion she made no attempt to quell.

She was falling for this man, her heart sang. She was falling in love with Jack MacAllister, who was real, and honest, and everything he claimed to be. Surely he would never betray her, lie to her. After all, she knew his truths, knew he would be leaving soon.

This night was hers.

She would bask in the wondrous glory of making love with a man with no secrets, no weapons of duplicity to destroy her with.

The memories would be hers to cherish once Jack was gone. Memories of a relationship that she would not have to bury deep within her to keep the pain from ripping her to shreds.

Oh, yes, this night was hers.

Jennifer shifted her hands to push lightly against Jack's chest, ending the passionate kiss. She got to her feet and, her gaze never leaving his, removed her clothes. She stood naked before him, the light from the dancing flames in the hearth cascading over her like a golden waterfall.

Jack's heart thundered as he strove for control. He made himself sit where he was, drinking in the vision of loveliness standing before him.

There she was, he thought hazily. Jennifer. *His* Jennifer. She was rendering herself totally vulnerable, trusting him, believing in him, knowing he would never hurt her.

And *he* trusted and believed in *her*.

Ah, yes, he truly did, because this was Jennifer, a woman like none he'd ever known before. An honest woman. A real woman. She didn't have a secret agenda, wasn't attempting to take from him more than he was willing, or able, to give.

No, not Jennifer.

She was simply Jennifer Mackane, exactly as she was, as he knew her to be.

And he loved her.

Jack stiffened, every muscle in his body tensing as the realization of his emotions slammed into his mind.

No! he thought frantically. How had this happened? When had he lost the tight command over his heart?

He had to get out of there, out of this house, put as much distance as possible between him and Jennifer as quickly as he could.

Run, MacAllister.

Run, before Jennifer discovered the true depths of his feelings for her, had the power to demolish him, strip him bare of all his defenses.

Go. Run. Now!

"Jack?" Jennifer said, her voice quivering slightly as a shadow of uncertainty clouded her features. "Don't...don't you want me?"

Ah, hell, Jack thought, he couldn't fight the spell Jennifer had cast over him. He couldn't leave her now, causing her to question his desire for her.

He couldn't do that—not to the woman he loved.

Jack rolled to his feet. "Want you? You'll never know how much."

Jennifer smiled. "Then show me."

Jack tore off his clothes, flinging them aside, then closed the distance between him and Jennifer. He took her into his arms, then lowered her to the floor and lay next to her. His mouth melted over hers, and a groan of need rumbled in his chest.

Jennifer splayed her hands on Jack's back, relishing the feel of his taut muscles beneath her palms.

Power. Strength, her mind hummed. But infinite tenderness, gentleness. Magnificent. Oh, how very magnificent was this man.

"Jack, please," she whispered, close to his lips. "I can't bear it. I need you. I want you...now."

"Yes. I've got to protect you, though, so—"

"No, no," she said, her hold on him tightening as a sob caught in her throat. "Don't leave me. It's all right. It's the wrong time of the month. It's safe. Don't leave me. Come to me, Jack. *Please.*"

All rational thought fled Jack's mind. He moved over her and thrust into her with one powerful surge, filling her.

It was wild. Earthy. Rough and real. The rhythm was pounding, the cadence thundering.

They were flung into oblivion seconds apart, holding fast to each other as they shattered into brilliant pieces. They lingered there, etching memories indelibly in their minds.

When they returned to reality, they didn't speak. They lay close, limbs entwined, sated and contented.

Jack moved finally to pull an afghan from the sofa to cover their cooling bodies.

Then with Jennifer's head nestled on Jack's shoulder, they slept.

Chapter Eleven

Jennifer peered into the oven, nodded in approval as she looked at the turkey, then closed the door. She turned to the counter and began to cut tomatoes into cubes for a salad while she hummed off-key.

Thanksgiving day, she thought. It was time to take a quiet moment and count her blessings—a pleasant task that would probably take more than all her fingers and toes to complete.

The sound of laughter reached her where she worked in the kitchen, and she smiled, knowing her home was filled with people who were important to her, people she loved.

Out in the living room, probably chattering like a magpie, was Joey, her precious son. It had been ten days since the frightening event of his surgery, and Joey was practically as good as new. He'd return to school on Monday, no doubt ready to relate his great adventure to anyone who would listen to the exciting tale.

Her beloved parents had driven up from Phoenix for the special day, and it was wonderful to see them. Andrea and Brandon were here, Aunt Prudence and Aunt Charity, Megan and Ben.

And Jack.

Jack, Jack, Jack, Jennifer thought, tossing a handful of tomato chunks into a bowl. The intensity and depth of her feelings for him grew with every passing day…and night, despite her knowing they had no future together.

She was an idiot. And she would pay a heavy price when Jack left Prescott, which he most certainly would.

All she knew for sure was that now, right now, she was happier, more fulfilled and complete, than she had ever been in her life. While Jack didn't know how she felt about him, she certainly did, and she was savoring every moment, every memory while Jack was still there.

The piper would come to collect his due when Jack was gone. She knew that, but still, she felt as she did.

"Football, football, football," Andrea said, coming into the kitchen. "We actually had some conversation going out there for a bit, but so much for that. The men are now watching other men clobber each other. What a silly game that is."

Jennifer laughed. "Don't let my mother hear you say that. She's a devoted fan of that nonsense. I told her that she likes to see guys wearing tight pants. She just smiled, and did *not* deny it.''

"Aunt Charity is watching the game, but Aunt Prudence is talking to Megan. I bet Aunt Charity takes a good look at those nifty male tushes, too.''

"I'm sure she does," Jennifer said, smiling. "What can I do to help you with dinner?''

"Nothing. It's all under control. With each of you bringing a part of the meal, there isn't that much for me to do. The turkey is cooking right on schedule. You and baby-girl Hamilton can just sit down at the table there and relax.''

"Baby-*girl* Hamilton?'' Andrea said, settling onto one of the chairs at the kitchen table.

Jennifer nodded. "No doubt about it. Jack told me about the MacAllister family baby bet and how Brandon qualifies because he's a close friend of a MacAllister. Brandon says you're having a girl, so—''

"I know, I know,'' Andrea said, laughing. "They made a believer out of me, too. I'm concentrating on the bachelor bet now. There are three candidates for marriage in the running—Jack, his brother Richard, and our own Sheriff Cable Montana.''

"So I've heard. Jack told me.''

"It would seem that Jack has kept you up to date on a lot of things, Jennifer.''

"Yes, well, I've been meaning to talk to you about Jack, but I never see you alone for long enough at the hotel.''

"Oh?''

Jennifer covered the salad bowl, put it in the refrigerator, then crossed the room and sat down opposite Andrea at the table.

"I'm all ears," Andrea said.

"No, you're all tummy," Jennifer said. "How are you feeling these days?"

"Fat," Andrea said. "Don't change the subject. What did you want to discuss with me regarding Jack?"

Jennifer took a deep breath and let it out slowly. "Okay," she said, "here goes. I know Ben must have told you that he saw Jack and me kissing in the waiting room at the hospital the day of Joey's surgery. And we were...kissing. Actually, you see, Jack and I are involved in a... What I mean is, we're— Now I realize it's very foolish because he'll be leaving soon, and I'll never see him again, but I don't care because I've never been this happy, and I'm holding fast to what I'm sharing with Jack for as long as it's mine to have."

Jennifer lifted her chin. "I don't want to hear that I'm headed for heartache because it's all temporary. I know the facts and I've accepted them, so don't worry about me. I just felt that since Ben told you what he'd witnessed at the hospital, I should explain that no one need be concerned that I'll be a basket case when Jack goes. Sad? Yes. Missing Jack? Oh, yes. But I'll be all right in time."

Jennifer nodded. "There. That covers it, I guess. Oh, wait. There's Joey, too. He's very fond of Jack, idolizes him, but we remind him that Jack will be leaving before Christmas. Joey seems to understand that. So, that's it. That should answer any questions you might have after Ben reported what he saw."

"I see," Andrea said slowly. "There's just one little thing you ought to know."

"What is it?" Jennifer said, frowning.

"Ben never said one word about seeing you and Jack kissing," Andrea said, laughing.

"Oh, good grief," Jennifer said. "I don't believe this. I was certain that he would go racing right over to the hotel and... Don't men know how to gossip?"

Andrea shrugged. "Some don't, apparently. Ben is a very private person, you know. Look how long he kept silent about the fact that he might lose his sight at some point in the future."

"That's true," Jennifer said, nodding. "Well, I just blithered my little heart out for no reason."

"I'm glad you told me, Jennifer, and I'm sincerely happy for you. I'm a bit worried, too, that you'll be hurt by this relationship because it will all be over soon."

"Nope. Won't happen. I won't be hurt."

"I hope you're right." Andrea paused, then nodded. "This explains why Jack... Yes, it makes sense."

"What are you talking about?"

"Well, I'll confess that we all had been discussing you a bit, wondering why you refused to even date. Jack presented a theory—this was early on, right after he'd met you—that maybe you weren't grieving for the happiness you'd had in your marriage with Joe Mackane, but were protecting yourself because that union had been...well, totally miserable."

Jennifer felt the color drain from her face. "Jack said that?"

"Yes, and it was something none of us had ever thought of," Andrea said, "due to the fact that you named Joey after his father."

"Yes," Jennifer whispered. "Yes, I did."

"Anyway, Jack got us all upset with that new thought and he promised to report back on any clues he got while he was repairing your house. Please don't be angry, Jennifer. This was all done because we care so much about you."

Jennifer nodded, still gazing at Andrea. Yes, she thought frantically, all of them *did* care about her, but, dear heaven, no, she didn't want anyone to know the truth about her and Joe Mackane.

"The thing is," Andrea went on, "Jack suddenly clammed up, wouldn't say a word, said it was actually none of our business. It was baffling because it had been his idea in the first place. Now everything makes sense."

"It does?" Jennifer said.

"Well, sure. Jack was becoming personally involved with you. Whatever had kept you from dating for the past five years was no longer standing in your way. But Jack, gentleman that he is, wasn't about to show up for breakfast at Hamilton House and announce to all of us that there was no longer any cause for concern about you because he was sleeping with you."

Jennifer's earlier pallor was replaced by a flush of embarrassment.

"I never said that we were—" she started.

Andrea laughed. "Hey, it's all right. I'm a big girl, know the facts of life. Of course you're sleeping with Jack." Her smile faded. "But, oh, Jennifer, I don't want to see you brokenhearted when he leaves.''

''I'll be fine,'' Jennifer said quietly. ''I really will. This time with Jack is like a gift I'm giving myself. I feel so womanly, so alive, so—''

''In love?'' Andrea said gently.

''Oh, no, no, I...'' Jennifer sighed. ''Well, truth is, I think I'm falling in love with Jack. I certainly didn't intend for that to happen, believe me, but I've accepted the reality of it and am prepared to handle it when he's gone.''

''Does Jack know how you feel about him?''

''Heavens, no,'' Jennifer said. ''There's absolutely no point in his knowing. In fact, it might be disastrous if he knew. He could very well break things off between us and leave for California earlier than he planned if he thought things were getting...sticky, shall we say, between us. No, he mustn't find out the depths of my feelings. I don't want to lose what time I have left with him—not one minute of it.''

''Oh, dear me,'' Andrea said, shaking her head. ''This sounds so emotionally...dangerous for you.''

''Worry not, my friend,'' Jennifer said, getting to her feet. ''I'm in control. All is right with the world. I've got to check on my turkey.''

As had been agreed, Brandon had brought a long, folding table from one of the conference rooms at the hotel, as well as enough chairs to seat Jennifer's guests. The table was set up in the living room behind the sofa that faced the fireplace.

Jennifer's parents had surprised her with a lovely

centerpiece of flowers in fall colors that looked perfect on the off-white linen tablecloth.

Jack's contribution to the event had been several bottles of top-of-the-line wine that Jennifer poured into crystal glasses. The table was filled with a variety of food, and delicious aromas floated through the air.

Jennifer sat at the head of the table with Jack on her right and Joey on her left, his plastic glass containing apple juice.

"A toast," Jennifer said, lifting her glass after everyone was seated. "To family."

"Hear! Hear!" Brandon said.

Jennifer clinked her glass against Joey's, then turned to repeat the ritual with Jack. He met her gaze and she smiled as their glasses touched. She forced herself to break the warm, visual contact with him, then spoke to her father, who sat at the opposite end of the table.

"Would you say grace, please, Dad?" she said.

Dishes were soon being passed and several conversations taking place at the same time. The noise level was high, the mood festive.

To family, Jack thought, mentally repeating Jennifer's toast. Yes, that was who was gathered around this table—friends who were so close and caring they were a family. It had been a great many years since he'd taken part in a traditional Thanksgiving like this one.

Family.

Jack slid a glance at Jennifer, then Joey, as he began to eat. He loved them. There was no point in attempting to deny it, nowhere to hide from the momentous truth of it. He loved Jennifer as a man loved a woman. He loved Joey as a father would a son.

The unanswered question was…what was he going to do about it?

Jennifer didn't have a clue as to his true feelings for her. He would leave for California just before Christmas as planned, with Jennifer none the wiser.

And that *should* be that. End of story.

But it wasn't, and he knew it.

He hadn't intended to fall in love with Jennifer Mackane, nor have his heart well and truly captured by her son, and he was angry as hell at himself that he had let it actually happen. A cold fist tightened in his gut as he once again questioned his inability to see the real agenda hidden by a woman.

But the thought of leaving Jennifer and Joey, walking out of their lives, never seeing them again, caused his stomach to clench yet again each time the image of their last goodbye flashed in his mind's eye.

Family.

His was waiting for him on the coast—the huge MacAllister clan, plus close friends who were included in the group. He'd be surrounded by those who loved him, overrun by little kids eager to spend time with fun-loving Uncle Jack. He'd have more than enough people to fill his idle hours.

Yet…

None of them would be Jennifer. None of them would be Joey.

His family. *His* wife.

Jack choked on a sip of wine as the word *wife* echoed loudly in his mind.

"Goodness," Jennifer said, reaching over and patting him on the back.

"It just went down the wrong way," he said, smiling slightly.

"I must say, Jack," Jennifer's father said, "that the old homestead looks great. I understand you're the one to thank for that."

"I helped Jack fix junk, Grandpa," Joey said. "We did men stuff together."

"So I heard," his grandfather said. "And a fine job you did, too, Joey. Have you and Jack finished with all your projects around here?"

"Yep," Joey said. "We're all done. Jack helped me make a birdhouse while I was 'cuperating from my operation, so it took him longer to do the house stuff 'cause he had to do it alone, but we're done now. Right, Jack?"

"Right, sport," Jack said. "We're a good team, you and I."

"Well, in my opinion," Jennifer's father went on, "this would be an excellent time to sell this place. It's spruced up and ready to go on the market."

"You're kidding," Jennifer said, halting her fork halfway to her mouth. "Sell our family home?"

"It's too big for you, Jennifer, and too difficult to maintain," her father said. "It's yours to do with as you wish, but your mother and I would like to see you and Joey living in something smaller, newer. Maybe a town house, where all the outside maintenance is taken care of by an association."

"But...but I grew up in this house," Jennifer

said, setting her fork back onto her plate. "And I could never accept money that belonged to you and Mom."

"Dear," her mother said, "your father and I have fond memories of the many years we lived here. All we're saying is, it's perfectly fine with us if you'd like to sell this rambling old place. Things change, and it's often best to let go of the past and look to the future."

"I don't know what to say," Jennifer said.

"Just think about it," her father said. "Thanks to…Joey and the help Jack gave our young man in repairing this place, it's market ready."

"Now you're talking," Aunt Charity said. "Let go of the past and look to the future. That's excellent advice, Jennifer."

"Yes, it is, dear," Aunt Prudence said.

"Joey?" Jennifer said. "Do you have an opinion about this?"

"If we moved someplace else," Joey said, "could I take my swing set?"

"Yes, of course," Jennifer said.

"'Kay." Joey shrugged, then shoveled in a mouthful of potatoes.

"It would complicate my life," Jennifer said. "I have such a good setup with Mildred Clark next door to tend Joey while I'm working."

"Mildred left yesterday to visit her daughter in Toledo," Aunt Charity said, "and won't be back until after the new year. Your routine is already blown to Timbuktu."

"Well, yes, I know," Jennifer said, "and I

haven't solved that problem yet, but... Goodness, actually sell this house?''

"Want us to vote on it, Jennifer?" Brandon said. "You won't have to get in a dither about it. We'll decide for you, wonderful folks that we are."

Jennifer laughed and shook her head. "No, thank you, Brandon. I need to give this some very serious thought. Let's change the subject to *your* house."

"Funny you should bring that up," Brandon said, smiling. "I just happen to have brought along the plans that Jack drew for us."

"Which you will all gush over, like it or not," Andrea said, smiling, "or Brandon will pout."

"You betcha I will," he said. "It's going to be a fantastic house. The contractor is ready to roll, and we break ground next week."

"Oh, congratulations," Jennifer said, smiling warmly. "That's so exciting."

"Well, Jack," Aunt Charity said, "sounds to me like you've wrapped up all your projects. What are you going to do with yourself, hotshot?"

Jack slid his hand across Jennifer's knee beneath the table. She jumped slightly at the sudden, tantalizing touch, and felt her eyes widen.

"Gosh, Aunt Charity," Jack said. "I don't know. I'll think of *something*."

"Thought you might, big boy," Aunt Charity said, cackling merrily.

Jennifer reached beneath the table and smacked Jack's hand where it still rested on her knee, causing him to burst into laughter.

"What's funny?" Joey said, frowning.

"Nothing, sweetheart," Jennifer said, hoping her

cheeks weren't as flushed as they felt. "Brandon, don't forget that you're taking turkey sandwiches to Cable Montana when you leave. I invited him to join us today, but he said that since he was single, he'd stay on duty and free up one of the married deputies."

"Nice save, Ms. Mackane," Jack said quietly, grinning at her.

"Hush, hush," Jennifer whispered, shooting him a quick glare.

Jack laughed again.

"What's funny?" Joey repeated louder.

"Not—a—thing," Jennifer said firmly.

"Ah, yes, Hunk-of-Stuff Montana," Aunt Charity said. "He's one of the candidates in the bachelor bet."

"Oh, boy," Jack said, frowning and shaking his head. "Here we go."

"I do believe," Aunt Charity said, tapping one fingertip against her chin, "that I'll plead senility and admit that I made a mistake when I put my money on Jack getting married. Yes, I'm officially withdrawing my wager."

Jack scowled and leaned forward so he could see Aunt Charity, who was farther down the table.

"Why?" he said.

"You're just not husband material, hotshot," Aunt Charity said. "Nope, I'm not blowing my cash by betting on you."

"I'm not husband material?" Jack said, his voice rising. "Why not? What in the—" he looked quickly at Joey "—heck is wrong with me?"

"Charity, dear," Aunt Prudence said, "I'm well

aware that our Jack wouldn't be what one might prefer to have in a husband, but I'm not certain that Thanksgiving dinner is the proper place to discuss it.''

''You feel the same way, Aunt Pru?'' Jack said, then slouched back in his chair. ''I don't believe this. Anyone else want to get on this bandwagon?''

''Well, now that you mention it,'' Brandon said, staring into space.

''Hey, I demand an explanation,'' Jack said. ''This is really rotten stuff you're laying on me here.''

''Jack would be a good groom guy,'' Joey said. ''He has a suit and tie, and everything.''

''Thank you, Joey,'' Jack said. ''I appreciate your support.''

''Uncle Brandon could teach you how to kiss so you could make a baby, Jack,'' Joey said.

''Oh, okay,'' Jack said, chuckling.

''Nope,'' Aunt Charity said. ''Jack isn't going to be a groom guy, Joey.''

''I repeat,'' Jack said. ''Why not?''

''You moved in the fast lane in New York City for too long, big boy,'' Aunt Charity said. ''Brandon got out of that scene in the nick of time, but you're hopeless. You're a love-'em-and-leave-'em type, no doubt about it.'' She shook her head. ''Can't see you mowing the lawn, taking out the trash, changing diapers. You're off to California to make whoopee with the beach bunnies.''

''What's 'whoopee?''' Joey said.

''I certainly am not,'' Jack said. ''I haven't given

one thought to the beach. Or the bunnies. I'm really getting insulted here.''

"Don't know why," Jennifer's father said. "Not everyone is cut out for marriage, Jack. That's just the way it is sometimes.''

"I'll have you know, all of you," Jack said, sweeping one hand through the air, "that I would be a dynamite husband." He nodded decisively. "I'm kind, thoughtful, would honor my wedding vows until the day I died. I could change a diaper if I had to…sure, I could do that. I'm handy around the house, could learn to pick up my socks and—"

Jack stopped speaking and glanced around the table. Everyone, except Jennifer, was smiling at him. Jennifer was simply staring at him with wide eyes, a rather stunned expression on her face.

"I've been had," Jack said, shaking his head. "I fell for it hook, line and sinker. You're a devious woman, Aunt Charity.''

"Just checking up on my twenty bucks," she said, looking extremely pleased with herself.

"I'm still not convinced that Jack is cut out to be a husband," Brandon said.

"Don't count your money yet, Aunt Charity," Megan said. "Just because Jack feels he'd be a good husband doesn't mean he wants to be one.''

"Bingo," Jack said, acknowledging Megan. "Got it in one.''

"That doesn't work, Megan," Ben said. "We men can be so dense on the subject of marriage that we oftentimes don't know that we want that kind of commitment, when in actuality we do.''

"Oh, brother," Jack said, rolling his eyes heavenward.

"Spare me."

"Would anyone like some pumpkin pie?" Jennifer asked, but no one paid any attention to her.

"You're right, Ben," Brandon said. "I'm a clearcut example of that theory."

"And look at you now," Andrea said, smiling as she patted her protruding stomach.

Brandon dropped a quick kiss on her lips. "I'm a happy man," he said. "Ecstatic. Over the moon and—"

"Give it a rest, Hamilton," Jack said gruffly.

"This is all very interesting," Jennifer's father said, stroking his chin, "and just confusing and complicated enough that I believe I'll pass on putting money on the bachelor bet in regard to Jack. I couldn't be certain which way to bet. Yes, this is *very* complicated."

Tell me about it, Jack thought. His poor muddled brain was dissolving into dust.

Marry Jennifer Mackane? Be a groom guy? A daddy bear? Oh, man, what a terrifying thought.

Or...or was it?

"Pumpkin pie with whipped cream?" Jennifer said, raising her eyebrows. "As in, we're changing the subject and concentrating on dessert? The topic of marriage has been known to give some people indigestion."

"Some people?" Jack said, no hint of a smile on his face. "Meaning you? I suppose you're with Brandon, agreeing with him that I'd make a lousy husband."

Jennifer turned her head slowly to meet Jack's frowning gaze. "No," she said quietly. "I think you'd make a wonderful husband, Jack." She paused. "Providing you found the right woman."

I have, damn it, Jack's mind yelled. *You! I love you, Jennifer Mackane. What's it going to take for you to trust and believe in me enough to love me in return?*

Oh, heaven help him, he *did* want to marry this woman, spend the rest of his life with her. And with Joey. And the children that he and Jennifer would create together while making sweet, sweet love in the darkness of night.

Jennifer switched her attention to the group. "Pie?" she said, her voice not quite steady.

"Yes," Andrea said quickly, "it's definitely time for pumpkin pie."

Jennifer got to her feet, picked up her plate and Joey's, then hurried into the kitchen.

Get a grip, Jennifer, please, she begged herself, putting the plates on the counter. She was rapidly losing the control that she'd assured Andrea she had.

Jack MacAllister in the role of a husband? Oh, yes. To a woman other than her? Oh, no. No, no, no. She couldn't bear the thought of his pledging his love forever to another woman.

She wanted Jack's forever to be with *her.*

Love, trust—they were emotions she'd sworn never again to have in regard to a man, but she wanted desperately to put her faith in Jack. To believe that he was different.

"Oh, Jennifer," she whispered, "you foolish, foolish woman. Now you want it all—and none of it is yours to have."

Chapter Twelve

Jack stood in front of the fireplace in Jennifer's living room, staring into the leaping flames. His hands were shoved into the pockets of his slacks and a deep frown knitted his brows.

That afternoon and on into the evening following the Thanksgiving dinner were a blur, he realized. No one had commented on the fact that he was acting strangely, so he must have performed in a halfway normal manner.

But the truth of the matter was, he'd been withdrawn, centered on his own raging thoughts.

Everything was happening too quickly, not allowing him time to adjust, to come to grips with the new and startling direction his life was taking.

He was in love for the first time. He'd forgotten the painful lessons about trusting too easily, believing that a woman was actually who she presented herself to be.

Oh, yes, he was, indeed, deeply in love with Jennifer Mackane.

Even more unsettling was the realization that he wanted to spend the rest of his life with her. Marry her, for God's sake. Be a groom guy for Jennifer, and a daddy bear for Joey.

Jack shook his head and sighed wearily. He needed to be alone, to get a handle on all this. The thought of a lifelong commitment terrified him, yet the idea of walking out of Jennifer's life forever was too chilling to bear.

"I'm a wreck," he said under his breath. "I'm totally losing it."

Jennifer stood at the entrance to the living room and stared at Jack, seeing the slump of his shoulders and hearing his deep sigh. He muttered something she couldn't make out, but she knew it was further evidence that he was troubled, upset.

He had been preoccupied since dinner, a fact of which no one but her, apparently, had been aware.

Had the silly conversation about the bachelor bet disturbed him? Jennifer wondered. Had Jack felt cornered when everyone focused on whether or not he was husband material?

Was he angry at himself for adamantly stating that he was very capable of being a good husband and father, when he had no desire whatsoever to function in either of those roles?

Oh, she didn't know what was on Jack's mind, knew only that he hadn't been himself since dinner.

The way to discover what was bothering him was to come right out and ask.

But she couldn't—wouldn't—do that.

She, too, had functioned on two levels since the Thanksgiving meal. Outwardly she had been cheerful, pleasant, an attentive hostess.

But another part of her had been struggling with the newfound truth that she wanted to spend the rest of her life with Jack MacAllister. Be his wife, the mother of his children, watch him perform in the role of Daddy Bear for her beloved Joey.

She wanted it all, and had fought against threatening tears throughout the seemingly endless hours that everyone was at the house, as her mind screamed unrelentingly that none of it was hers to have.

No, she couldn't ask Jack what was troubling him. It was too risky. Suppose, just suppose, that despite his own preoccupation he'd been aware of hers? What if he returned the question, wanted to know what had been wrong with *her* in the hours following dinner?

So much for communication between a man and a woman, Jennifer thought dryly. She was breaking one of the important rules of being in a relationship, but she had no choice but to keep silent.

Jennifer lifted her chin and walked farther into the living room. "Joey's asleep," she said, forcing a lightness to her voice. "He had such fun today, but he's thoroughly worn out."

Jack turned from staring into the flames and looked at Jennifer. "That's good," he said. "I mean, it's not good that he's worn out, but it's good that he's asleep, getting his rest and... Never mind.''

Jennifer sat down on one end of the sofa. ''Would you like some coffee, Jack? Brandy? There's some of that wine you brought left, too.''

''No. No, I'm fine, thank you.''

You are not fine, Jack MacAllister, Jennifer thought. Oh, what, what, what was troubling him?

''I—I hope you enjoyed yourself here today, Jack,'' she said.

Jack slouched onto the sofa, rested his head on its back and looked at the ceiling. Jennifer slid a glance at him and registered the distance he'd put between them. A cold knot tightened in her stomach.

''It was really great,'' Jack said, still staring at the ceiling. ''It's been years since I've been part of a traditional Thanksgiving celebration. It was...very nice.'' He paused. ''Tiring, though. All that chatter and... Wipes a person out.''

''Well...''

Jack turned his head to look at Jennifer. ''Aren't you exhausted?'' he said.

''Well...''

He lunged to his feet, and Jennifer jerked in surprise.

''Sure you are,'' he said. ''Listen, I'm going to shove off and let you relax, then get to bed early. Okay? Yeah, good idea.''

Oh, Jack, Jennifer thought, feeling the sting of tears in her eyes once again. *What is wrong?*

She got to her feet.

''All right,'' she said, hoping, praying that her voice was steady.

"I—I'm going to drive down to Phoenix tomorrow, Jennifer," Jack said, directing his attention to the fire again. "I've never been there, and I'd like to take a look at some of the historical buildings. I might...might stay a couple of days. It's a big city. Lots for an architect to take in. You know?"

Lame, MacAllister, he thought. But he needed some time alone to make sense of the jumbled mess his mind had become.

"Yes," Jennifer said softly. "Phoenix is very big city. Very big."

Jack nodded, then strode across the room to the front closet and retrieved his jacket. Jennifer walked toward him slowly and met him at the front door.

He dipped his head and brushed his lips over hers. "I'll call you, or come by, when I get back to Prescott," he said.

Jennifer nodded, unable to speak past the ache of tears in her throat.

Jack looked directly at her, an intense but unreadable expression on his face. He lifted one hand and drew his thumb gently over her cheek.

"Ah, Jennifer, I..." he started, then stopped speaking and shook his head. "Good night."

"'Night," Jennifer managed to whisper.

Jack left the house, closing the door behind him with a *click.* Jennifer snapped the lock into place, then leaned her forehead against the smooth wood and allowed the pent-up tears to flow.

Jennifer was scheduled to work days starting on the Monday following Thanksgiving, requiring her to be at the hotel at seven a.m. and leave at 4:00 p.m.

Due to Mildred Clark's vacation, Jennifer made arrangements to drop Joey off at Sammy's house in the early morning.

Joey would attend a day-care center adjacent to his school after kindergarten was dismissed, a fact Joey was reserving judgment on until he—to quote—checked it out for fun stuff to do.

As Jennifer seated the breakfast patrons, she made a silent wish that this Monday would be one of the days Andrea, Brandon and the aunts would decide to eat in their own apartments upstairs in the hotel.

She did not want to explain to the observant quartet why she had purple smudges beneath her eyes from lack of sleep. She was also certain that her plastic-feeling smile would not fool the caring foursome.

Jennifer sighed, acutely aware of her bone-deep fatigue. She'd tossed and turned the night Jack announced he was going to Phoenix. And she'd tossed and turned every night since, her sleep coming in short doses that produced muddled, yet definitely disturbing, dreams.

Jennifer frowned and stared into space, recalling how happy she had been as the Thanksgiving festivities began, and how miserable she'd been by the time the special day was over.

This was a practice run, she supposed, for when Jack packed up his vehicle and headed for California in just a few weeks. And, oh, mercy, it was awful, just terrible, and lonely beyond belief.

Well, no, she reasoned in the next instant, this was

different than that final leaving would be. Jack's sudden decision to go to Phoenix had not been on the schedule.

There was something troubling Jack, and she'd made no attempt to communicate with him, to discover what was causing his turmoil, due to her fears that he might demand similar answers from her.

Jack's exodus to the valley with so much left unsaid between them was admittedly as much her fault as his.

She was once again being pulled back into the painful memories of the past, nearly numb with the fear that Jack would somehow hurt her, shatter her, with what he refused to share. She was losing her trust and belief in him, those newly found emotions slipping through her fingers like grains of sand.

Jennifer smiled automatically as a couple entered the dining room and made the appropriate, pleasant remarks as she led them to their table and handed them their menus. When she returned to the podium, she narrowed her eyes and stared into space again.

No, by golly, she was *not* going to step backward into the dark world where she'd existed with Joe Mackane. She'd moved into the sunshine with Jack MacAllister and was stronger for it, free of the hideous ghosts of lies and betrayal. She would not be beaten by old fears.

If Jack contacted her upon his return from Phoenix—oh, please, let Jack contact her when he got back to Prescott—she was going to sit him down and talk to him, for heaven's sake. If she truly believed in him, trusted him, then it was time to prove it—not only to him, but to herself as well.

That baring of her soul wouldn't change the outcome of her relationship with Jack. She knew that. He would still leave Prescott before Christmas. All that they'd shared would be over, forever. She was prepared to deal with that.

But she would handle it as a woman changed, as one who had grown, become stronger, had reached into the dark shadows of her past and retrieved the very essence of who she was to be complete now, whole.

But she couldn't say that final goodbye to Jack with dignity and grace if she didn't step up and square off against whatever it was that was now taking place. Whatever was wrong with Jack—and, therefore, with them—had to be addressed.

It had to be done in order for her to be who she wished to be. Free of the horror of the past. A woman of strength, courage and purpose. A woman who would cry when Jack left, but one who would have the fortitude to dry those tears and move forward with her life.

"Hi, Jennifer."

Jennifer jerked at the sound of a woman's voice. "Hello, Deborah," Jennifer said, smiling. "I haven't seen you in ages. How are you?"

"Busy," Deborah said. "I'm meeting some clients who are staying here at Hamilton House. We're having breakfast, then I'm going to show them some houses. They're ready to retire and have decided that Prescott is the place to settle and enjoy."

Jennifer glanced at the reservation book. "Yes, here you are. A table for three. Do you want to wait here for your people, or be seated now?"

"I'll sit and have some coffee," Deborah said. "I'm facing a lot of hours on my feet today. I wish I still had the energy I did when you and I were in high school together. Anyway, my clients are the Reynolds. You can send them in my direction when they arrive."

"Very good."

Jennifer led Deborah to a table, gave her a menu, and placed two more on the table for the expected couple. "Enjoy your breakfast," Jennifer said, then started away.

She stopped, took a deep breath and returned to stand next to Deborah. "I want to sell my house and I'd like you to have the listing."

Deborah's eyes widened. "You want to sell—You're kidding. You grew up in that house. I can still recall the hours we spent together in your nifty room on the top floor when we were in high school. Remember how we pretended we were in our own apartment in whatever exciting city struck our fancy that day?"

"Yes, I remember," Jennifer said, "but the house is too big for me and Joey, and is impossible to maintain. Thanks to a—a friend, everything is repaired right now, spruced up. This is the time to sell… It was my folks' idea and…well, I'm going to do it. I want a nice-size town house with a backyard big enough for Joey's swing set. I hope you can find us something."

"Well, I'm definitely surprised," Deborah said, "but thrilled to have the listing. I shouldn't have any trouble selling a beautiful historic home like yours. I'll call you to set up a time when I can come by and do a walk-through and settle on an asking price. Okay?''

"Fine," Jennifer said. "Thanks."

"Thank *you*," Deborah said, smiling. "You made my day. I'm a happy Realtor."

And she, Jennifer thought, walking away, was as stunned as Deborah. During the long days and nights since Thanksgiving dinner, her subconscious must have been busily dwelling on her parents' suggestion that the family home be sold. She'd been so centered on Jack, she'd had no idea that part of her was working through the question of whether or not to sell the house.

Well, fine. So be it. Being involved in a muddled mess of a relationship was good for something other than sleepless nights. She would have driven herself crazy wondering what to do about her home, but had now discovered she'd made the decision already. She'd just opened her mouth and told Deborah to put the house on the market.

And it felt right. It truly did. It was one more step forward, instead of lingering in the past.

Oh, yes, indeed, she was changing and growing, gaining an inner strength she had no idea she possessed.

And when—well, *if* Jack MacAllister showed up on her doorstep after driving back up the mountain, they were going to talk, by golly, openly and honestly, even if she had to bar the door and keep him in her living room until she'd had her say.

Jennifer nodded decisively, and when the next people entered the dining room, her smile was genuine.

* * *

The evening Jack returned to Prescott, he stood across the street from Jennifer's, one shoulder propped against a large tree as he stared at the house.

He'd managed to avoid seeing Andrea, Brandon and the aunts when he'd returned to Hamilton House, thank goodness.

A quick glance into the dining room, then some idle chitchat with the guy on duty at the registration desk gained him the information that Jennifer was working days and had left the hotel at four o'clock.

So here he was, skulking in the shadows. Any second now, he thought, the cops were going to arrive, blue lights flashing, sirens wailing, after receiving a report of a suspicious-looking man who was hugging a tree.

Jack glanced again at his watch, which he could see clearly in the glow of the street lamp. Five more minutes, he decided. It had been ten minutes since the light in the bedroom he knew to be Joey's had been extinguished. He was waiting to be certain the little boy was sound asleep before he knocked on Jennifer's door.

It wasn't that he didn't want to see Joey, because he did, he really did, but this wasn't the time for a fun romp with Joey—not by a long shot.

Jack dragged both hands down his face and sighed wearily. Man, he was beat. Hadn't had a decent night's sleep since before Thanksgiving. In the hotel in Phoenix, he'd done more pacing and thinking than sleeping, and when he had managed to doze off, it had been a restless slumber.

Enough was enough, he'd finally concluded. He couldn't go on like this. The time had come to have a serious discussion with Jennifer, to sit her down, to tell her that he was in love with her.

It wouldn't be what she wanted to hear, that was for damn sure, but he was going to unburden his beleaguered brain, be certain that she listened, even if he had to block the doors of the house with furniture.

It could very well be that Jennifer would tell him to take a hike, to hit the road, to get out of her life. His declaration of love might rob him of the remaining weeks left to be with her.

But that was a risk he was going to have to take because the jumble of emotions within him was more than he could handle.

And the fact that he wanted to be Jennifer's groom guy and Joey's Daddy Bear? A husband and father? Every time he focused on that realization, his mind just stopped. That was due, he knew, to the cold-fist-in-his-gut feeling that he'd never get that far in baring his soul to Jennifer.

He'd broken the rules of their no-strings, no-commitment relationship. Man, had he ever. Jennifer liked the agreed-upon status quo, the end of which would be a breezy "See ya, Jack" as he set off for California.

Oh, yeah, he was about to burst Jennifer's blissful bubble, gum up the works big time. Jennifer wanted no part of a forever with him because...

Jack frowned and straightened from his slouching pose against the tree.

...Because Jennifer Mackane had secrets from her

past that were dictating her present, and robbing her of a future.

And she didn't trust and believe in him enough to share those secrets with him. That hurt. That really ripped him up.

He'd overcome his own self-doubts about his ability to really trust Jennifer, to be certain she didn't have a hidden agenda, but she hadn't returned in kind that kind of heartfelt, emotional trust. Damn.

Jack looked at his watch again, then drew a deep breath, letting it out slowly. "Okay, MacAllister," he said aloud. "This is it. Get geared up to be sent packing."

Chapter Thirteen

When the knock on the front door reverberated through the living room, Jennifer jumped to her feet, then sat down abruptly as a wave of dizziness assaulted her. She blinked, placed one hand on her racing heart, then rose again slowly.

Jack was here, she thought, walking toward the door. She knew, just somehow knew, that he was standing on her front porch. So, okay, fine. This was it. Truth time.

"I'm not home," she said under her breath. "Oh, Jennifer, get a grip. You can do this. You *have* to do this."

She lifted her chin, squared her shoulders and opened the door.

"Hello, Jennifer," Jack said quietly.

Jennifer drank in the very sight of him. She'd

missed him so much, she wanted to fling herself into his arms and—

"Jennifer?"

"Oh! Yes, hello, Jack," she said, stepping backward. "Come in."

Jack moved past her, took off his jacket and dropped it onto a chair, then went to stand in front of the fire, where he rubbed his hands together.

Jennifer stared at him, then jerked herself back to attention and closed the door. She returned to her spot on the sofa, acutely aware that her legs were trembling and her heart was racing.

Jack turned from the fire and met her gaze. "How are you, Jennifer?" he said. "And Joey? How's Joey?"

"We're both fine. Did you enjoy your trip down to Phoenix?"

"No."

"You didn't?" Jennifer said, frowning. "Then why did you stay away so long?" She paused and shook her head. "Oh, listen to me. I might as well come right out and say that I missed you. I did…miss you."

"I missed you, too." Jack stared at the ceiling for a long moment, then looked at Jennifer again. "What I'd like to do is take you in my arms and kiss you until we can't breathe. Then? Then we'd make love for hours, not talking, definitely not talking—just…just feeling."

Go for it, MacAllister, Jennifer thought giddily, as a frisson of heat whispered through her.

"But I can't do that, Jennifer, because we *have*

to talk. There are things that need discussing, can no longer be ignored.''

''I know,'' she said quietly, clutching her hands in her lap.

''We made a pact of sorts,'' Jack went on, ''that contained the ground rules of our relationship. We had an understanding that no one could get hurt because we both knew the facts, acknowledged that all this was temporary.''

''Yes.''

''Well, Jennifer, I broke the rules, and I can't go on with everything bottled up inside of me. It's driving me nuts. I have to be honest with you, tell you the truth, knowing full well that by doing so you might choose to end things between us right now.''

''I...I don't understand, Jack. I mean, I broke the rules, too, but I don't for one minute believe that you broke the same rules that I broke and— Oh, I'm not making any sense.''

''What rules did you break?'' Jack said, frowning.

''What rules did *you* break?'' she said, matching his expression.

''Hell, this isn't getting us anywhere,'' he said, his voice rising.

''Shh. You'll wake up Joey, and this is obviously an adult conversation.''

''No joke.'' Jack shook his head. ''Whew. This is rough going. Okay. Jennifer, I've been hurt in the past, disillusioned time after time because of my choices in relationships, because of the women I trusted and believed in. I was wrong, duped, every damn time. They all had hidden agendas, something they wanted from me...materialistically, socially, whatever. None of them were real. None of them were who they presented themselves to be. Never again, I vowed. Never, never again.

"Then I met you. I waited, watched, listened for your…your program, for what you were really after by agreeing to engage in a relationship with me."

"But I—"

"Please." Jack raised one hand. "This is difficult enough. Let me finish."

Jennifer nodded, her eyes holding Jack's.

"As each day…and night…went by," he continued, "I began to realize that you *didn't* have a secret agenda. You *are* real. You *are* honest. You *are* who you present yourself to be."

"Yes. Yes, I am, but you sound angry about it. This is very confusing, Jack."

"You think *you're* confused? I'm eligible for Olympic Gold in that category," he said, splaying one hand on his chest. "Why? Because you made me break my promise to myself, forget the past and what I'd supposedly learned from it. Because you…because you're you and… Damn it, Jennifer, I fell in love with you!"

"You did? Oh, you did not." Jennifer's eyes widened. "You did?"

"I did. I am." Jack dragged a hand through his hair. "In love. With you. That's the part of the rules I broke." He paused. "Ah, hell, what a mess. If you want to end things between us right here, right now, I'll understand because—"

"No," she said, her voice unsteady. "This all terrifies me at the same time that it makes me happier than I've ever been in my entire life. I intended to tell you how I felt if you came to me when you returned from Phoenix. I was so afraid you'd leave for California sooner than planned, but I knew I had to tell you. I'm falling in love with you, too.''

''I—''

''It doesn't mean that I think we have a future together, or anything like that,'' Jennifer rushed on. ''But I couldn't keep silent any longer because I wouldn't be true to myself if I did. I—''

''Wait a minute,'' Jack said, slicing one hand through the air. ''Wait just a damn minute here. You're saying that you're falling in love with me?''

''Yes,'' she whispered.

''On the surface, that sounds like two pieces of a puzzle fitting together, doesn't it? But there's a helluva big piece missing.''

''There is? What piece is missing? You're confusing me again, Jack.''

''Trust and belief, Jennifer. Your trust and belief in me is *not* in this picture. I've told you about my past, about why I was determined not to become seriously involved with a woman again. I spelled it all out for you. But you? You have secrets, Jennifer. There is something about your marriage to Joe Mackane that made you vow never to love again, never to remarry. There's a whole section of yourself that you won't allow me to touch, share.

''You say that you're falling in love with me,'' he continued, ''but how can that be true when you don't trust and believe in me enough to tell me what happened between you and Joey's father? Maybe you had the greatest marriage imaginable and couldn't fathom being able to come close to that kind of perfection again, so you didn't intend to even try. But I don't think that's the case—not even close. Tell me, Jennifer. Tell me about your existence with Joe Mackane.''

Jennifer nervously crossed her arms and held her elbows for a moment, then dropped her hands to her lap again. ''No.''

Jack sat down next to her, shifting so he could lay one arm across the top of the sofa behind her. He covered her hands with his other hand, and she turned her head to meet his gaze.

''Ah, Jennifer, don't you see?'' he said. ''Your past is standing between us like a solid wall. We can't acknowledge, can't…embrace the fact that we're meant to be together, let alone gather the courage to think about what the future might hold… Talk to me. Share with me. Trust and believe in me the way I do you.''

''Are you testing me?'' Jennifer said with a sudden flash of anger. ''Is this one of those 'If you really love me, you'll do this' things?''

Jack looked away and stared into the fire for a long moment, then met Jennifer's gaze again. ''Yes, I guess I am testing you,'' he said. ''I'm so unsure of myself on the subject of being in love. I know that I love you, but, oh, man, it scares the hell out of me. I'm trying desperately to get a handle on my emotions here, be comfortable with them, welcome them. I'm no expert on love, but I do realize that this secret of yours is too big, has too much power. We're fragile, Jennifer, very fragile in this new place we've found ourselves. There's no room in here for your ghosts. Do you understand what I'm saying?''

Jennifer drew a wobbly breath. "Yes. Yes, but... Oh, God, no one knows what happened with Joe. I haven't told anyone—not even my parents. I have to protect Joey from the truth. He must *never* discover the true facts about his father."

"Do you think I'd ever do anything to hurt Joey?"

Jennifer looked into the depths of Jack's dark eyes. "No," she said softly. "No, you wouldn't."

"And you?" Jack said. "Can you envision me hurting you, Jennifer?"

"No."

"Then tell me about Joe Mackane."

Jennifer got to her feet and moved to stand in front of the fire. She stared into the flames, her hands once again wrapped protectively around her.

Please, Jennifer, Jack pleaded silently, staring at her. *Please talk to me.*

They couldn't do anything until the ghosts—the barrier—created by Jennifer's past were gone.

Talk to me, Jennifer, please.

"When I graduated from college," Jennifer said quietly, still staring into the fire, "I took a position as the manager of a small hotel in Colorado. When I'd been there about six years, a construction crew came to town to do the finishing work on a retirement home project. There was a lounge—a bar in the hotel that was popular with the local people. Joe and the other men in the construction crew came into the bar on a regular basis."

Jennifer turned slowly to look at Jack, and he frowned as he saw that the color had drained from her face.

"Joe swept me off my feet," she said, her voice flat and low. "He made me feel beautiful, special, like the most important woman on the face of the earth. I was so…so unsophisticated and inexperienced and…I fell in love with him—or believed I was in love—and two weeks after I met him we were married. I was twenty-seven years old, but a young, unworldly twenty-seven, and Joe was thirty."

Jack nodded.

"I wanted a church wedding with my parents present, wanted to be married here in Prescott, but Joe said he couldn't get time off from work and he'd meet my mother and father later. We were married by a justice of the peace with office workers as witnesses, then moved into a tiny apartment."

Jennifer stopped speaking and stared into memory-filled space.

"And?" Jack prompted, hardly breathing.

"After a month of wedded bliss," Jennifer went on, "Joe said the job he was on was completed and he'd taken a new assignment out of town, two hundred miles away. He'd only be able to get home on the weekends. I wasn't happy about it, but I put on a brave face—wanted to be the perfect, supportive wife.

"I kept busy at work and lived for the weekends when Joe would be home," she said. "But he began to make excuses why he couldn't come—they were working overtime, he had the flu…whatever. I had to wait for him to telephone me, because he said there was no phone in the boarding house where the crew was staying."

Jack narrowed his eyes.

"I was lonely, so lonely," Jennifer said, shaking her head. "Then I found out that I was pregnant. Oh, how thrilled I was about the baby, could hardly wait to tell Joe. I was determined not to share my news over the telephone. It was too special, too wonderful. Or...so I thought."

"What happened?" Jack said quietly.

"Joe was gone for over a month after I discovered I was pregnant. When he finally came home, I fixed his favorite dinner, put candles on the table, dressed up so prettily for him. As we ate, I told him about the baby. He...he was furious. He said I was supposed to have made certain I wouldn't get pregnant. He didn't want any part of being a father, and I should terminate my pregnancy immediately."

"Ah, Jennifer," Jack said. "I'm so damn sorry."

"Oh, that's just the tip of the iceberg, Jack," she said, a sudden bitter edge to her voice. "This story gets even better. I refused to end the pregnancy, and Joe came home less and less, often staying away two months or more at a time. He wouldn't touch me when he did show up because he said I was fat, disgusting."

"Why—why didn't you divorce him?"

Jennifer pressed her fingertips to her temples. "I couldn't admit to myself that I'd made such a terrible mistake marrying Joe. I convinced myself that he'd change his attitude once he saw and held our baby."

"Jennifer," Jack said, extending one hand toward her.

"No," she said, her voice trembling. "Let me

finish. I'm hanging on by a thread here. Don't— don't comfort me, or I'll fall apart."

"Don't say any more," Jack said, getting to his feet. "This is too painful for you. It's okay, Jennifer. We'll just leave it in the past where it belongs. We won't allow it to stand between us."

"No, I'm going to get it all out," she said, her eyes filling with tears. "I need to. It's been festering within me for so long, consuming a part of me that I want back. Yes, I need to do this."

"All right," Jack said, remaining on his feet.

"A week before the baby was born," she said, looking directly into Jack's eyes, "one of the men from Joe's construction crew came to the apartment. He told me that Joe had been killed when a wire holding a high platform let go and Joe fell to the ground. I was devastated. My parents flew up to be with me and we were informed that funeral arrangements had already been made. I didn't question that. I was numb—in shock.

"On the day of the funeral it rained," she said. "I don't know why I'm telling you that, except that at the time it seemed to represent my life—so bleak and dark. After the graveside service, a woman in her late forties asked to speak to me alone. My parents went on to the car, and I stood there with that stranger, that woman, next to Joe's casket."

"Who was she?" Jack said, his heart racing.

A sob caught in Jennifer's throat. "Joe's wife! Are you getting this, Jack? *She was Joe's wife.* She sneered at me, said I was a stupid child, just one more in a long string of affairs that Joe had had. She didn't care if he played around, she said, because he always came home to her. And then she laughed, Jack. She laughed. She said Joe had really done it up big this time by actually going through with a marriage ceremony. He did love a challenge, she said, and had probably gotten a real kick out of seeing if he could pull it off.''

"That lousy son of a—" Jack started, then shook his head.

"The baby was a joke on Joe, the woman said, still laughing that horrible laugh,'' Jennifer said, "and it would have served him right to get stuck with child support. She left me standing there in the rain. I could hear her laughter as she walked away— heard it in my nightmares for months afterward… My world was shattered. It had all been lies, a joke, a game. I was so ashamed. How could I have been so gullible, so foolish, so—"

"Jennifer, don't," Jack said. "It wasn't your fault. You couldn't have known that Joe—"

"I trusted and believed in him," she said, tears spilling onto her pale cheeks, *"and he destroyed me."*

"Damn it," Jack said, rubbing a hand over his face.

"I vowed, as I stood there in the rain staring at Joe's casket, that no one, *no one,* would ever know the truth. No one would know my shame. And even more important, I would protect my child from the truth of the kind of man his father really was."

"And so you named your son after his father," Jack said, "to indicate a—a memorial of love and respect and… You named the baby Joey."

"Yes," Jennifer said, dashing the tears from her

cheeks. "But when I look at my son, say his name, I have no thoughts of Joe, of what he did, who he really was. Joey is mine. He has no...no connection to Joe Mackane. None. Joey will never learn the truth about his father."

A sob caught in Jennifer's throat and fresh tears filled her eyes. She lifted her chin and drew a deep, shuddering breath.

"So, did I pass your test, Jack?" she said, tears once again streaking her cheeks. "Did I get high enough marks? Are you satisfied now?"

"Oh, Jennifer."

Jack closed the distance between them and pulled Jennifer into his embrace, holding her tightly. She buried her face in his shoulder and wrapped her arms around his waist as she struggled not to cry.

"I'm so sorry," Jack said. "I shouldn't have pushed you to relive that pain. I've been so selfish, deciding how things should be between us, demanding that you...Jennifer, please forgive me for putting you through this ordeal. I love you, and I've hurt you, and I'm so damn sorry."

Jennifer raised her head to look at Jack, and he nearly groaned aloud as he saw the tears glistening on her pale cheeks and shimmering in her beautiful, green eyes.

"No, you didn't hurt me, Jack," Jennifer said, her voice trembling. "You were right. The past is over. It's the present and—and the future that matters. I do trust and believe in you. I do...love you."

Jack attempted to reply, but sudden, overwhelming emotions closed his throat. He shook his head slightly, then captured Jennifer's lips in a heartfelt kiss that he hoped would convey the words he was unable to speak.

Jennifer returned the kiss in total abandon, joyously aware that she was, at long last, free of the haunting, painful memories that had plagued her for so many years. She was free to live and free to love.

And as unbelievable and wondrous as it seemed, Jack loved her in return.

Jack gently broke the kiss, then wiped away Jennifer's tears with a stroke of his thumbs.

"Pretty heavy stuff, huh?" he said, his voice raspy.

"*Very* heavy." She smiled, then sniffled. "Very special. Very scary."

"Yep. Look, I have a suggestion to make," Jack said. "I'm sure as hell not saying this is how it has to be, because my dictator days are over after what I just did to you. But, I just think…maybe we shouldn't discuss the future yet—not yet. Let's give ourselves time to adjust to the idea that we've fallen in love. How does that sound?"

No, Jennifer thought. It was wrong. It meant she still had a secret, was still keeping something of great magnitude from Jack that might cause him to reconsider and end things between them now. She needed to tell him that she wanted it all—a forever with him. Wanted to be his wife, wanted him to be a father to her son.

"Okay?" Jack said. "Jennifer?"

"Yes, all right," she said. "We'll live in the present for now, savor it and how we feel about each other, because we're free of the past."

"We'll live one day at a time."

"There aren't that many days left before you're scheduled to leave for California, Jack."

"There's plenty of time," he said, lowering his head toward hers. "Plenty—" he brushed his lips over hers once "—of time—" twice "—my love." Then his mouth melted over hers in a feverish kiss.

A shiver of foreboding coursed through Jennifer, but was quickly replaced by the rushing current of desire that consumed her.

Chapter Fourteen

Time.

It was such a small word, Jennifer thought, staring at the calendar on the kitchen wall. It had only four letters and rhymed with lime, and slime, and chime and…

Time, her mind echoed over and over. Time…time…time…

It was moving too fast. It hardly seemed possible that it had been nearly three weeks since the night she had told Jack the truth about Joe Mackane.

Three weeks since she and Jack had declared their love for each other.

Three glorious weeks of sharing, caring, making love.

Three weeks with not one word spoken by either of them about the future.

Time was rapidly ticking away, while screaming the fact that there were only ten days left until Christmas, the holiday that Jack was scheduled to spend in California with his family. She'd been so centered on Jack that she now realized she hadn't heard word from Deborah about putting the house on the market.

Jennifer sighed, glanced at her watch, then began to pace restlessly across the kitchen.

Up until this very moment, she'd wanted time to stop, leaving her suspended in the wondrous world that revolved around Jack and Joey.

But right now? she thought, looking at her watch again. She wanted the next four minutes to fly, instead of dragging by second by second the way it was.

In four more minutes—no, in three minutes and thirty-five seconds—she would hurry down the hallway to the bathroom and check the results of the home pregnancy test she'd taken.

"Oh, dear heaven," she said, stopping her trek and pressing her fingertips to her aching temples. Stay calm, she ordered herself. She was *not* pregnant. Her body was off-kilter, reacting to stress and fatigue. She'd taken the test to reassure herself of that fact, to put the ridiculous notion to rest once and for all.

She—was—not—pregnant.

She was exhausted, the pace at work having increased to a near-frenzy. Hamilton House was booked solid through the holidays, the nightly number of patrons in the dining room growing.

There were also endless private parties being held

in the conference rooms, events that required Jennifer to check and double-check a multitude of details, ensuring everything was ready.

There was Christmas shopping to complete, gifts to wrap, cards to be addressed and mailed. One entire, memory-making evening had been spent with Jack and Joey, buying a tree, setting it up in front of the living room windows, then decorating it as they played carols on the stereo.

Adding to her fatigue was the fact that she hadn't been sleeping well. In the dark, quiet hours of the night, the underlying tension and stress hovering around her and Jack reared its nagging head and screamed her doubts and fears over Jack and his intentions.

Despite his declaration of love, did Jack still plan to walk out of her life before Christmas? Was her love, her trust and belief in Jack MacAllister misplaced? Was he going to shatter her hopes, her dreams, her heart by leaving her forever?

Oh, Jack said he loved her, but did he wish to spend the rest of his life with her? Did he want to be her husband, and a father for Joey?

The questions were there, always there, demanding more attention with each passing day.

No wonder her body was out of whack, she thought, throwing up her hands. She'd had several dizzy spells because of the building stress she was under. Her appetite was nonexistent, and when she did eat she became queasy.

But no, she wasn't pregnant. She was a woman in love who had to know what the future held. What was called for here was another serious discussion with Jack.

"Definitely," she said decisively, then looked at her watch. "Okay. Time is up."

She marched from the kitchen, her eyes narrowed as she envisioned sitting Jack down that night after Joey was asleep and telling Mr. MacAllister that enough was enough. They had to talk about their future together—or lack of same.

She'd wasted precious money buying the pregnancy test kit, Jennifer thought as she approached the bathroom. She didn't have a nickel to spare during the holidays aside from what she spent on presents for everyone on her long list.

With a cluck of self-disgust, she entered the bathroom and went to the vanity where she'd placed the pieces of the kit.

And then she stopped breathing.

Her heartbeat pounded painfully in her ears. Tiny black dots danced before her eyes, and she gripped the edge of the sink with both hands as she stared at the little plastic device.

"Oh, God," she whispered, "no. It's wrong. A mistake. This isn't true." She drew a wobbly breath, and a bubble of hysterical laughter escaped from her lips. "Yes, it is. I'm pregnant. I'm carrying another baby who might not be welcomed by its father. Dear heaven, what am I going to do?"

With trembling hands, Jennifer collected the pieces of the kit, stuffed them into the box, then hurried back down the hallway. In the kitchen she shoved the box into the trash basket, hiding it under a layer of debris.

Then she sank onto a chair at the table, rested her elbows on the place mat and dropped her face into her shaking hands.

Jack's baby, her mind thundered. She was pregnant with Jack MacAllister's baby. How had this happened? They were always careful. Jack protected her every time they made love and—

Jennifer raised her head and her eyes widened. *One night.* There had been one night when she had clung to Jack, hadn't wanted him to leave her even for a moment. It had been after the horrifying ordeal of Joey's surgery. She had been physically exhausted and emotionally drained, had wanted only to escape to the blissful place Jack took her when they made love.

She had almost forgotten about that passion-filled night. She now remembered that she'd told Jack it was all right, it was the wrong time of the month for her to become pregnant—and that had been true. But her body obviously hadn't been paying attention to the calendar.

And she'd conceived Jack's child.

Jennifer sank back in the chair and splayed her hands on her flat stomach. Jack's baby, her mind whispered. No, it was *her* baby. Her secret. She was not going to tell Jack about this child unless he came to her and asked her to marry him. She wouldn't trap him into proposing to her, thus sentencing herself to a lifetime of wondering if he truly wished to be by her side.

If Jack packed up and left, went to California per his original plan, he would never, ever know that this child existed.

And the serious discussion with Jack that she'd scheduled on the agenda for this evening? Oh, yes, they'd have that talk, but she'd keep a tight rein on her emotions, be very certain that she didn't blurt out her news of the baby. She'd wait to hear what Jack had to say.

Wait…while she hoped and prayed that he'd ask her to be his wife. Then, and only then, would she tell him about this baby.

Jennifer stiffened as she heard the sound of the front door, accompanied by Joey's chatter. She got to her feet, produced what she felt was a passable smile and went into the living room.

"I bought your Christmas present, Mom," Joey said, jumping up and down. "It's wrapped and everything. You can't peek at it, either."

"Oh, it's beautiful," Jennifer said, smiling. "Why don't you put it under the tree?" She looked at Jack, who was shrugging out of his jacket. "You survived shopping with Joey, I see."

Jack tossed his jacket onto a chair, then turned to look at Jennifer, a frown on his face. "Yeah, it was fun," he said. "Joey has champagne tastes on a beer budget, though." He paused. "We bumped into a woman named Deborah while we were in one of the stores. She recognized Joey and asked me to give you a message."

"Oh?"

"She said you knew she'd been called out of town on a family emergency, but she had just gotten back and hoped to show your house to prospective buyers very soon."

Jennifer shrugged. "Okay. That explains why I

haven't heard from her. Thank you for telling me. Why don't you two gentlemen wash up, because I have a casserole in the oven for dinner and it should be ready in about five minutes.''

"'Kay,'' Joey said, running from the room.

Jack walked slowly toward Jennifer, his frown still firmly in place. ''You didn't tell me that you'd definitely decided to sell this house,'' he said, sweeping one arm through the air as he stopped in front of her.

''I didn't?'' Jennifer said, matching his frown. ''I thought I'd mentioned it. I made up my mind right after Thanksgiving, but you were in Phoenix and... Oh, well, nothing has happened about it because Deborah was called away. But she's back now so...'' She shrugged again.

''You're awfully casual about such a major decision in your life, Jennifer. If you sell this house, you'll need a new place to live.''

''Well, yes, that's generally how it goes, but to tell you the truth, I've been so busy I haven't given the whole subject much thought.''

''To tell me the truth,'' Jack said, his frown deepening. ''Interesting premise. Damn it, Jennifer, don't you think I had the right to know that you intended to sell your home and start over somewhere else? Just where do you believe that somewhere will be?''

''I don't have a clue,'' she said, planting her hands on her hips. ''Nor do I have the slightest idea what you're pitching a fit about. I'm obviously missing something here. Would you care to enlighten me, Mr. MacAllister?''

"Washed my hands," Joey said, racing back into the living room. "I'm hungry. Can we eat now?"

"Yes, of course." Jennifer shot a glare at Jack before directing her attention to her son. "You can help me set the table while Jack washes his hands." She spun around and headed for the kitchen. "Come on, Joey."

He was definitely losing it, Jack thought as he walked slowly down the hallway to the bathroom. He'd felt his tension building as each day went by, bringing him closer and closer to the time he was scheduled to leave for California. There was a knot in his gut that kept coiling more and more tightly.

In the bathroom, Jack scrubbed his hands, dried them, then studied his reflection in the mirror mounted above the sink. It wouldn't have surprised him to see that he'd grown a couple more heads, each containing a brain that was focused on a different subject.

One part of him was in heaven. Being with Jennifer, knowing she loved him as he loved her, was fantastic, out of this world. During the past weeks they'd operated as a family—Jennifer, Jack and Joey. Mommy bear, daddy bear and baby bear. Perfect. He was so content and happy in his roles that his feelings defied description.

But there was another part of him that felt like a ticking bomb that was counting down the days, hours, minutes, seconds until he had to gather his shaky courage and ask Jennifer to marry him. He wanted her and Joey to leave Prescott, come to California with him, be part of the new life he would start there.

What if Jennifer refused his proposal? What if she said no? What if she smashed his heart to smithereens and sentenced him to a bleak, empty, lonely existence without her?

And then there was the third brain, the ugly one that refused to completely disappear. It had a voice, that brain, that taunted him, told him not to let down his guard like a fool, but to be on alert for the possibility that Jennifer did, indeed, have a secret agenda.

It had been that part of his mind that had reacted to the previously unknown news that Jennifer had decided weeks ago to sell this house.

Why hadn't she told him? Was she envisioning a huge new home on the coast, with him picking up the tab? Was she breathing a sigh of relief that her days of standing on her feet for long hours as the manager of the dining room at Hamilton House would soon be over if she became a lady of leisure at his expense?

"Damn," Jack said aloud, dragging both hands down his face. How could he even entertain such rotten thoughts about the woman he loved? The woman he *knew* was real and honest. The woman he trusted and believed in.

He'd been so sure that he'd put his past behind him, just as Jennifer had, but there was a dark shadow left within him that still claimed a part of his soul.

"What are you going to do, MacAllister?" he said, leaning toward the mirror. "Walk out of her life, or ask her to go with you?"

Jack left the small room and headed for the

kitchen, his thoughts tumbling one into the next, creating a jumbled maze of confusion.

He loved Jennifer Mackane and intended to spend the rest of his life with her.

But why hadn't she told him she'd put her house on the market?

Jennifer believed in him, trusted him with her heart—the very essence of herself—and with her precious son.

Or was the total abandonment of her lovemaking and her urging him to spend time with Joey part of a master plan to snag herself a financially secure husband and a devoted father for Joey?

Ah, hell, he couldn't go on like this. Not only was he running out of time on the calendar, he was slowly but surely losing his sanity, as well.

Tonight. Yes, tonight after Joey was asleep, he was going to have a serious discussion with Jennifer. Tonight, decisions would be made that would determine the course of their futures. This was the night.

Jack entered the kitchen to find Jennifer talking on the telephone and Joey hopping up and down like a pogo stick beside her, a big smile on his face.

"All right," Jennifer said into the receiver. "Forty-five minutes. I'll try to get some dinner into him before you pick him up. 'Bye."

Jennifer replaced the receiver and looked at Joey. "Halt," she said. "Sit. Eat."

"'Kay," Joey said, then ran to the table and slid onto his chair.

"What's going on?" Jack said.

"That was Sammy's mother on the phone," Jennifer said, not looking directly at Jack. "The families on their block are going Christmas caroling, and they invited Joey to go, then spend the night with Sammy.''

''Oh,'' Jack said, nodding.

''Hurry, hurry,'' Joey said. ''I gotta eat and pack my stuff.''

''We'll have to bundle you up good,'' Jennifer said. ''It's starting to snow outside. Isn't that fun, Joey? Singing Christmas carols in the snow.''

''Neat-o,'' Joey yelled. ''Cool.''

''Cold,'' Jennifer said. ''You keep your mittens on, young man.''

'''Kay.''

They consumed the meal hastily, then Jennifer left the kitchen with Joey to help him pack for the sleep-over and to put on the layers of clothes for the outing.

Jack began to clear the table. As he scraped the food from a plate into the trash, he frowned as he saw that the liner in the basket was full. He pulled it free, tied a knot in the top and headed out the back door, flipping on the backyard light as he went.

The snow was falling in big, wet flakes, turning everything into a winter wonderland.

As Jack swung the bag up to place it in the large container provided by the city, the bottom of the liner struck the edge and split, spilling trash onto the ground that was becoming rapidly covered with snow.

''Ah, hell,'' he said, hunkering down to scoop up the debris. Then his outstretched hand stilled and his heart began to race in a wild cadence. With visibly shaking fingers he picked up the box that announced in bold letters Home Pregnancy Test Kit. He shook the contents onto the ground, looked at the plastic device, then flipped the box over to read the chart on the back.

"Positive," he said. "Holy hell, Jennifer...Jennifer is pregnant."

A red haze of fury and heartfelt pain assaulted him, making it difficult to breathe. He flung the scattered trash into the container and slammed the lid, his breathing labored, his motions jerky. He cleaned his hands with the freshly fallen snow, then attempted to dry them on his damp jeans.

Then he turned and stared at the house that suddenly seemed to be miles away, out of his reach, disappearing into oblivion and leaving only the dark, chilling emptiness of betrayal behind.

You're a natural-born father, Jack.

We're in this together, Jack.

It's the wrong time of the month. It's safe. Don't leave me. Come to me, Jack. Please.

You're a natural-born father...natural-born father...natural-born...

"No!" Jack said, his voice raspy. "Oh, God, Jennifer, no."

Lies. It had all been lies. Jennifer Mackane was like all the others. She'd had a secret agenda the entire time they'd been together, had set out to trap him and—

The back door of the house was flung open, and Joey poked his head out. "'Bye, Jack," he said. "I'm going singing in the snow now."

"What? Oh, have a great time, sport."

"See ya," Joey said, then slammed the door.

"See ya," Jack said quietly.

He started toward the house, struggling to put one foot in front of the other. He felt drained, and had to tell himself to breathe in, then out.

He entered the kitchen, vaguely aware that he was tracking wet snow onto the clean floor. He closed the door, leaned against it, then drew a shuddering breath.

"'Bye," Jennifer called in the distance. "Have fun. I love you, Joey."

Jennifer was smiling when she returned to the kitchen, but frowned when she looked at Jack. "My goodness," she said, "you're all wet. What have you been doing?"

"I—I took out the trash," Jack said quietly.

"Oh. Well, thank you. Why don't you go in by the fire and dry off? I'll take care of this mess from dinner and join you in a few minutes. You might catch a cold if you stand around in those damp clothes."

"Once a mother, always a mother," Jack said gruffly, starting across the room. "Right, Jennifer?"

"I…" she said.

"I'll be in the living room."

Jennifer watched Jack disappear from view, then began to clean the kitchen. Jack was still acting strangely, she thought. Was he brooding about her not telling him she'd decided to sell her house? Why was he making such a big deal out of something she'd simply forgotten to mention?

Maybe she was reading too much into Jack's behavior. He was cold and damp at the moment and was probably grumpy because of it. She was so jangled, due to discovering that she was pregnant, that she wasn't capable of thinking clearly. Yes, that was it. *She* was the one who was upset—not Jack.

When she joined him in the living room, he'd be his usual chipper self. And she'd tell him that they needed to have a very serious discussion.

What she would *not* tell him was that she was carrying his baby—*unless* he first asked her to marry him.

What transpired with Jack this evening would determine her entire future.

When the kitchen was clean, Jennifer drew a steadying breath, then went into the living room. Jack was standing in front of the fireplace, staring at the leaping flames. She settled onto the end cushion of the sofa, then splayed one hand on her stomach for a moment.

"Jack," she said, "we need to talk."

He turned slowly toward her, a closed expression on his face.

"Yes," he said, nodding, "we do. Go ahead. I'm listening."

"Well, time is running out," Jennifer said, clasping her hands in her lap. "There's only a week or so left before you'll be leaving for California."

"Yep," he said, folding his arms over his chest. "I've promised everyone that I'll be there for Christmas, for the reunion."

"Yes, I know." Jennifer paused. "Jack, these weeks we've had together have been wonderful. We agreed not to discuss the future, but the days are passing so quickly that the future is becoming the present."

"Mmm," Jack said, nodding.

"You're scheduled to leave, and I need to know what you're thinking about us, about..." Jennifer threw up her hands and sighed.

"At the risk of sounding like Aunt Prudence," Jack said, "you want to know if I have honorable intentions regarding you. Right?"

"That's one way to put it, I guess," Jennifer said, frowning slightly.

"Isn't there something you need to tell me at this point, Jennifer?" Jack said, narrowing his eyes.

"No," she said slowly. "Only that I love you very much."

"Damn it, Jennifer," Jack yelled, shifting his hands to his hips, "knock it off, would you? Enough is enough. I know what your agenda is, so give the game-playing a rest."

"I don't know what you're talking about," Jennifer said, getting to her feet. "Why are you so angry? Why are you shouting at me?"

"You heard me say that I took out the trash. Didn't it occur to you that my clothes and hair were awfully wet for a quick run to the trash container and back?"

"I—"

"The bag broke, spilling trash into the snow," Jack said, his volume still on high. "I picked up the junk—and guess what I found? A handy-dandy, home pregnancy test kit with a plastic deal that was still registering the big news."

"Oh, dear heaven." Jennifer sank back onto the sofa as her knees began to tremble.

Jack strode forward and braced one hand on the

arm of the sofa, the other on the top, trapping Jennifer in place. She leaned back instinctively as Jack loomed above her, a muscle ticking in his jaw.

"When did you plan to tell me that you're pregnant with my baby?" he said, his voice low and harsh. "Were you holding your trump card until you found out if I intended to ask you to marry me? And if I'd said, 'Well, it's been a helluva fine time, sweetheart, but I'm outta here,' were you going to whip your newsflash on me? Push my buttons, yank my strings like I was a marionette? Try to force me to marry you? When, Jennifer? When did you plan to inform me that you're carrying my baby?"

Jennifer flattened her hands on Jack's chest and shoved him away. He straightened, and she scrambled to her feet, immediately spinning around to face him, her green eyes flashing.

"I wasn't going to tell you at all," she said, nearly yelling, "unless you asked me to marry you. I had no intention of doing what you're accusing me of doing."

"Yeah, right," he said, his voice ringing with bitterness. "You put your house up for sale so you'd be ready, footloose and fancy-free when it came time to go to California with me. Ah, yes, *me*, the 'natural-born father' of the century. You've been sliding that little zinger in every chance you got. And if I refused to marry you despite your being pregnant? Well, hey, just go to plan B. Hire a sharp attorney and soak me for every dime you could get in child support."

"No!" Jennifer said, shaking her head. "If you didn't love me enough to want me to be your wife, to stay by your side until death parted us, then you would never have known about this child. It would be *my* baby. Mine. Just as Joey is mine with no connection to Joe."

"Damn it, Jennifer, you're insulting my intelligence. Oh, that's a hoot. My intelligence. I was such a fool, just like I've been with every woman I've ever been involved with. I even fell for your 'It's the wrong time of the month for me to get pregnant' crap. You're slick, Jennifer, very good. You had me under your spell, knew it, and everything fell right into place for you."

"No, Jack, you're wrong," Jennifer said, unwelcome tears filling her eyes. "How can you say such horrible things to me? I thought you loved me, believed in me, trusted me, as I did you. You're betraying my love and trust in your own way, just as Joe did in his. Dear God, Jack, don't do this to us."

"Don't try to lay a guilt trip on *me,*" he said. "*You're* the one who's so conveniently pregnant. I'm just the idiot who bought into your phony facade. Well, nice try, lady, but you lose. Oh, you'll get your child support money, but you're not snaring me in your matrimony trap."

Jack laughed, the sound sharp and humorless. "Want to know the kicker? I'd planned to ask you to marry me. I wasn't sure what I was going to do, but I know now that I wouldn't have been able to leave for California without you and Joey. Well, forget it, Ms. Mackane. I'm going to the coast *alone.*"

"Fine. You do that," she said, wrapping her hands around her elbows. "Don't bother to send child support checks, because I'll tear them up. I don't want anything from you, Jack MacAllister. Nothing.''

''You can't keep my child from me if I decide that I want to be part of his life. That decision will be mine—not yours. I'll make that clear to your attorney when I'm contacted about how much I'm to shell out to you every month.''

''Stop it!'' Jennifer shrieked, shaking her head. ''You're destroying everything we've had together.'' Tears spilled onto her cheeks. ''You're not even leaving me the memories I thought I could cherish. I trusted you, Jack, believed in you and, equally important, I believed that you trusted me. I—'' A sob caught in Jennifer's throat, choking off her words.

''Don't bother turning on the tears,'' Jack said. ''They won't work this time. I'm leaving, Jennifer. I'm leaving this house, this town.''

He looked up at the ceiling for a moment, struggling to regain control of his emotions. He looked at Jennifer again, and when he spoke his voice was a hoarse whisper. ''Damn it. Why couldn't you have been real?''

Jack snatched up his jacket from where he'd tossed it onto the chair and strode to the door.

''Jack,'' Jennifer said, tears echoing in her voice.

He stopped, his back to her, one hand gripping the doorknob.

''I *am* real,'' Jennifer said. ''I know that I didn't set out to get pregnant, despite what you believe. I know that my love for you is genuine. None of that matters to you now, but I'll seek solace in those truths. I won't keep you from being a part of your child's life if you choose to be, but I will *not* accept one penny from you. I have to think of Joey, too. Would you meet him after school tomorrow and walk him home, say a proper goodbye? Don't break his heart, too, by just disappearing from his world."

"Yeah, I'll walk him home tomorrow."

"Thank you. You won't have to see me again. Just leave Joey on the porch after you bring him home. I'm back on the evening shift at the hotel starting tomorrow, but I imagine you'll be gone by the time you might join Andrea and Brandon and the aunts for dinner." Another sob caught in Jennifer's throat. "Goodbye, Jack."

Jack's hand on the doorknob began to tremble and he muttered an earthy expletive. He yanked open the door and left the house, slamming the door closed behind him.

Jennifer gave way to her tears, allowing them to flow freely down her face and along her neck. The distance to the sofa was too far to walk, would require more energy than she possessed.

She sank to her knees on the floor, wrapped her arms around herself and wept from the very depths of her soul as her heart shattered into a million pieces.

Chapter Fifteen

"No!" Joey burst into tears and flung his arms around Jack's neck. "I don't want you to leave, Jack. Please don't go away. I don't want to have to give you back the way I do Uncle Brandon and Uncle Ben. No, no, no."

Jack rose from his hunkered position on the sidewalk leading to the porch of Jennifer's house. He lifted Joey into his arms as he straightened, holding him tightly.

As Joey buried his face in the crook of Jack's neck and cried, a knot tightened in Jack's gut and an achy sensation burned his throat. "Don't cry, sport," Jack said, his voice husky. "You knew I would be going to California before Christmas. I have a lot of miles to drive."

"You don't have to go," Joey said, his voice

muffled. "You can draw pictures of houses here. You can stay with me and my mommy, Jack. You can. We could be a real family, just like Sammy has, and you could kiss my mom so we could get a baby, and—"

"Joey, stop it," Jack said.

This bundle in his arms was tearing him apart, Jack thought miserably. He'd known this farewell was going to be rough but, oh, man... He was exhausted, had hardly slept the night before as he'd replayed that final scene with Jennifer over and over in his mind. He was emotionally drained, sliced and diced, and now Joey was pouring salt in his raw wounds.

"Come on, partner," Jack said. "Don't cry."

"I have to cry 'cause I'm sad," Joey said, then sniffled.

Jack set the little boy on his feet and pried his arms free. "Okay, you're right," Jack said. "There's nothing wrong with crying when you're sad. But that doesn't mean that the tears will change how things are. I really do have to go, Joey."

Joey swiped his nose across the sleeve of his jacket, then glared at Jack. "No, you don't," Joey said. "You want to leave, that's what. You like me and my mom, but you don't love us, 'cause if you did you'd stay with us. I love you, Jack, and my mom does, too. I know she does, 'cause she smiles at you all the time with the special smile that makes her eyes happy. How come you don't love us back?"

"I..." Jack started, then stopped speaking and shook his head. He *did* love Joey, as much as any man could love his own son. And Jennifer? He loved the woman he'd believed she was before her duplicity came to light. "Go into the house, Joey. It's cold out here."

"No."

"Yes. Go on. I'll never forget you, sport. You'll always be my buddy."

Joey stomped toward the house, his unhappiness emphasized by every heavy step he took. Jack watched until Joey had gone inside and slammed the door, then turned and walked slowly away, his heart aching.

I love you, Jack, and my mom does, too…smiles at you all the time with the special smile that makes her eyes happy.

I trusted you, Jack, believed in you and, equally important, I believed that you trusted me.

We could be a family, just like Sammy has.

I won't keep you from being a part of your child's life if you choose to be, but I will not accept one penny from you.

I don't want to have to give you back the way I do Uncle Brandon and Uncle Ben.

I know that I didn't set out to get pregnant, despite what you believe. I know that my love for you is genuine.

Jack stopped and pressed his fingers to his temples.

How long would he be tormented by Jennifer and Joey's words?

How long would he hear their voices, and see both of them so vividly in his mind?

How did a man forget a little boy who had captured his heart?

How did he live with the pain of being betrayed by the only woman he had ever loved?

Jack sighed and started off again, finally arriving at Hamilton House. When he entered the lobby of the hotel, he saw Andrea standing by the huge, decorated Christmas tree by the front windows. He quickened his step, not wanting to engage in a conversation with her—or anyone, for that matter.

"Jack?" Andrea said.

Damn, he thought, halting in his tracks. "Hi," he said quietly as he turned to face her.

Andrea came over to where Jack stood and frowned as she studied his face. "What's wrong?" she said finally. "You look like you just lost your best friend."

"Got it in one," Jack said, attempting to produce a smile, but failing miserably. "Two of them, in fact." He paused. "Listen, I'm heading out, leaving for California as soon as I get packed. I have a Christmas present for Joey in my room, and I was wondering if you would give it to him for me?"

"Why can't you do it yourself?" Andrea said.

"Because I've already said goodbye to him."

"I didn't realize that you were planning on leaving so soon, Jack. I mean, I thought that you and Jennifer were…" Andrea's voice trailed off.

"Yeah, well, things aren't always what they appear to be, are they?" he said, an edge to his voice. "To be more precise, people aren't always who they present themselves to be."

Andrea narrowed her eyes. "Are you referring to Jennifer?"

"Never mind," Jack said wearily. "There's nothing to be gained by rehashing the whole thing. I made a mistake. End of story."

"Yo, MacAllister," Brandon called. He crossed the lobby to join Jack and Andrea. "What's happening?"

"Jack is leaving this afternoon," Andrea said.

"You are?" Brandon said. "Why?"

"Because he's convinced he made a mistake by falling love with Jennifer," Andrea said.

"Hey, wait a minute," Jack said. "I never said that I was in love with Jennifer."

"Oh, for Pete's sake," Andrea said, "how dumb do you think we all are? Any idiot who sees you two together would know you love each other."

"*I* could even tell," Brandon said. "And I have a tendency to be a tad slow on the uptake about these things. The way Jennifer looks at you, smiles at you, Jack? Oh, yeah, she loves you—and, I will add, you love her."

"Just drop it, okay?" Jack said. "Don't go there. It's complicated and... Bottom line? It's over."

"Because Jennifer wasn't who she presented herself to be?" Andrea said.

"Yes!" Jack said, none too quietly. "I have to go pack."

"Don't—you—move," Andrea said.

"Uh-oh," Brandon said. "You're really in for it now, buddy."

Andrea pointed to a grouping of chairs in the lobby. "Sit, Mr. MacAllister."

"Hell," Jack said, then strode to one of the chairs and slouched at the edge of it. He unbuttoned his jacket and glared at Andrea and Brandon as they sat down opposite him. "Where's the bare lightbulb?"

"It can be arranged," Andrea said. "All right, give me one example of how Jennifer isn't who she presented herself to be."

Jack leaned forward and rested his elbows on his knees. "Okay. Try this on for size. Do you know that Jennifer plans to sell her house?"

"Yes," Andrea said, nodding. "She gave the listing to Deborah, who hasn't had time to put up a sign on Jennifer's lawn because there was a family emergency. Deborah is back now, though."

"Oh," Jack said. "Yeah, well, I bet Jennifer didn't happen to mention where she intends to live once her house is sold."

"I'll take that bet," Brandon said. "Jennifer told Deborah she wanted a town house for her and Joey so the outside maintenance would be taken care of."

"Oh," Jack said, frowning. "She said that?"

"Yes, Jack, she did," Andrea said, staring at him intently. "And if she said it, then it's true. Jennifer places a tremendous amount of importance on honesty."

"Right," Jack said dryly, leaning back in the chair again.

"Jack, let me tell you something," Andrea said. "I confronted Jennifer on Thanksgiving, asked her if she was in love with you. She said she was falling in love with you, but wasn't planning on telling you because she was afraid you'd leave Prescott earlier than scheduled. She wanted to share every possible moment she could with you. Jennifer knew that you'd leave before Christmas, but she was willing to run the risk of having her heart broken. She allowed herself to be totally vulnerable because of how much she loved you. She assured me that she would handle it just fine when you left, but I've been so worried that she wouldn't…''

Jack's gaze was riveted on Andrea, and his heart thundered, echoing in his ears.

''Oh, Jack, don't you see?'' Andrea said gently. ''Jennifer's love for you is so real, so pure and honest, that her own potential heartache was unimportant compared to what she was sharing with you. Jennifer wasn't who she presented herself to be? She isn't capable of being anyone other than herself. She just doesn't know how.''

Jack drew Andrea's softly spoken words deep within himself, then waited for the cacophony of voices, bringing the doubts, the evidence of betrayal, the pain.

But they didn't come.

The cold chill within him was replaced by an incredible warmth, a soothing touch of peace and understanding that caressed his mind. Though it had taken some very special friends to knock some sense into him, in his heart and soul he knew the truth about Jennifer. And the error of his ways.

''Dear God,'' he said, his voice husky with emotion, ''what have I done? I accused Jennifer of—I was so sure that she had— My fears created by my past had a louder voice than the truth of Jennifer's love for me and…I've lost…*I've lost the only woman I've ever loved.*''

"That's what I thought once myself," Brandon said quietly, "but I was wrong. Women in love are incredible creatures, Jack." Brandon got to his feet, then extended one hand toward Andrea to assist her from the chair. "You blew it?" Brandon said. "Then fix it, buddy."

"Go to her, Jack," Andrea said. "Give Jennifer a chance to forgive you."

Jennifer threw back the blankets on the bed with a disgusted click of her tongue. She shoved her feet into her Big Bird slippers and left the bedroom, unable to sleep and refusing to lie there and toss and turn for another moment.

Four-thirty in the morning, she thought, entering the living room, and she'd only had snatches of sleep. She couldn't go on like this. She was consumed by images of Jack, memories of Jack. His smile. His touch. His masculine aroma and rumbly chuckle. His beautiful chocolate fudge sauce eyes. His—

"Jennifer, shut up, please," she said aloud.

After her eyes adjusted to the darkness, she wandered over to the Christmas tree, then her glance fell on the drapes covering the remainder of the windows not filled by the tree.

Look at the sidewalk, Jennifer, she told herself. *See that it's empty. Jack isn't there. He'll never be there again. He's gone...forever.*

Jennifer brushed aside the curtain, then gasped at the same moment she felt her heart begin to beat a rapid tattoo.

Jack was standing on the sidewalk! There he was,

in the same spot she'd first seen him so many weeks ago. Jack was there.

He was hunched against the cold, his hands shoved into the pockets of his jacket. It was snowing lightly, and the street lamp cast an eerie glow in the snow-filled darkness.

Jennifer dropped the curtain and pressed trembling hands to her cheeks. Get a grip, she told herself. There was no way on earth that Jack MacAllister was really standing on that sidewalk at four-thirty in the morning in the freezing cold. Her imagination and heartfelt desire to see Jack had conjured up an image of him that wasn't real. Jack was in California, no doubt sleeping soundly after the long drive to the coast.

"Rest, Jennifer, you need rest," she said. "You're slipping over the edge."

She turned from the drapes, then hesitated.

All right, she thought. Just one more teeny, tiny peek to prove to herself that she was once again in control. Jack was *not* standing on that sidewalk. And after that nonsense was settled, she was going back to bed.

She moved close to the curtains and opened them just enough to peer out with one eye. "Oh, dear heaven," she whispered, "he's still there."

Her breath caught as the ghostly figure of Jack pulled one hand from his pocket, waved, then pointed toward the front door of the house.

As though her head did not belong to her, it nodded in agreement, and the mirage on the sidewalk started toward the house.

Jennifer dropped the edge of the curtain and

smoothed her nightshirt neatly over her hips. Poor Joey, poor new little baby, she thought rather hysterically. Their mother is a cuckoo.

Jennifer snapped on a lamp, then went to the front door and unlocked and opened it. The next instant she slapped both hands over her mouth to stifle a scream.

Filling the doorway was an enormous furry brown teddy bear wearing a suit and tie.

"May I come in? Please?" the bear said. "I'm frozen solid."

Jennifer heard a funny-sounding giggle, then realized it had come from her. "Well, certainly," she said, stepping back. "Never let it be said that I allowed a bear to freeze to death on my front porch."

The bear entered the room, and Jennifer closed the door.

As she turned, she saw Jack set the bear on the floor, then straighten and smile at her. "Hi," he said.

"If you think that I intend to carry on a conversation with a figment of my imagination," Jennifer said with an indignant sniff, "you're crazy. Correct that. *I am* crazy and I've had enough of this malarkey. I'm going back to bed. Goodbye."

"Jennifer, wait," Jack said, raising one hand. "You're not imagining that I'm here. I'm real."

"Don't be ridiculous. Why would you be standing on my sidewalk, transforming yourself into a six-foot Popsicle at four-thirty in the morning?"

"Actually," Jack said, "I've been out there since about three o'clock. I couldn't sleep, needed to see and talk to you the minute you woke up so..." Jack shrugged. "It seemed like a good idea at the time but, damn, I'm cold."

Jennifer reached out tentatively with one finger and poked Jack in the chest. "Merciful saints," she said, her eyes widening, "you *are* real."

"Could I start a fire in the hearth so I can defrost?"

"Go for it," Jennifer said, then looked at the bear. "I suppose that bear is really here, too."

"Yep."

Jack went to the fireplace and began the process of making a fire. Jennifer studied the huge bear for a long moment, shook her head slightly, then followed Jack across the room and sank onto the sofa.

As the flames began to crackle in the hearth, Jack closed the screen and turned to look at Jennifer, all traces of his smile gone.

"I had to see you, Jennifer," he said quietly. "Talk to you. I've come here to tell you how much I love you and to beg your forgiveness for what I did. I said some lousy things to you, hurt you terribly, which is something I had vowed never to do. I was wrong, so damn wrong, and I'm more sorry than I'll ever be able to express to you in words."

Jennifer sank back against the sofa cushion, her gaze fixed on Jack.

"I was so determined," Jack went on, "that you put your past to rest, be free of your ghosts, that I wasn't aware that I hadn't finished dealing with my own. When I found out that you planned to sell this house, then discovered that you were pregnant, I was flung back in time—couldn't see, or think, beyond the memories of all the women who had duped me."

"But I—"

"But you," Jack interrupted, "are not like any of those women. You're open, and honest, and exactly who you present yourself to be. I know…now…that you didn't set out to trap me into marriage by getting pregnant. I know now that your decision to sell this house wasn't part of a secret agenda, a master plan of deception. You put the pain of your past behind you—and I have finally done the same. Oh, Jennifer, I love you so much. I want to spend the rest of my life with you, with Joey, with our baby you're now carrying, and three or four more little MacAllisters."

Tears filled Jennifer's eyes, and she had to remind herself to breathe.

"I guess you're wondering about that bear," Jack said. "He's sort of…tangible evidence of what I'm attempting to say to you. I want to be a groom guy, wearing a suit and tie. I want to be the daddy bear when we create a family. I trust and believe in you, Jennifer, I swear I do… Jennifer, please forgive me. Please. Say you will, and say you'll be my wife. *Oh, God, Jennifer, please.*"

Jack opened his arms to her.

Jennifer flew off the sofa and into his embrace. He staggered slightly from the impact, then wrapped his arms around her so tightly that it was as though he'd never let her go again.

"Yes," Jennifer said, "I forgive you. Yes, I'll marry you. Oh, Jack, I love you beyond measure."

"Thank you," he said, drawing a deep breath of relief. "Will you move to California with me?"

"Of course." Jennifer paused. "There's just one thing that we need to discuss."

"What is it?"

"How many little MacAllisters did you say we should produce?"

Jack chuckled, and Jennifer shivered at the wonderful, familiar, masculine sound.

"One at a time, my love," he said. "How's that?"

"Perfect."

Jack lowered his head and captured Jennifer's lips in a kiss that spoke of commitment, of pain dealt with and dismissed for all time, of love that was rich and deep, honest and real.

"You're kissing my mom!"

Jennifer and Jack jerked apart, breaking the kiss, but Jack continued to hold Jennifer close to him.

Joey jumped up and down in excitement. "You are," he said. "You're kissing my mom, Jack. We're going to get a baby. We're going to be a family. Right? I won't ever have to give you back, will I, Jack?"

"No, Joey," Jack said, smiling. "You won't ever have to give me back."

"Neat-o!" Joey yelled. "Wow! Look at that big teddy bear. Cool."

"You can have him," Jack said, "because I'm going to be a *real* groom guy and daddy bear." He shifted his gaze to Jennifer again. "We're going to be together."

"Forever," Jennifer whispered, smiling through her tears. "Forever."

*   *   *   *   *

*Turn the page
for a sneak preview of*

**THE BABY BET:
HIS SECRET SON,**

*a Silhouette single title
by beloved author
Joan Elliott Pickart,*

on sale July 2000.

Whose guest was *he?*

He was the epitome of the clichéed tall, dark and devastating man. Wide shoulders, broad chest, long, muscular legs and rough-hewn features.

And he was so intent on his scrutiny of the people in the room, he hadn't even noticed she was standing there.

Kara cleared her throat.

The man continued his perusal of the room.

"Happy New Year," she said brightly and fairly loudly, "and welcome to the party."

The man's head snapped around and he frowned as he stared at her.

She extended her right hand. "I'm Kara Mac-Allister," she said, "and I'm the welcoming committee at the moment. May I ask your name and enquire as to whose guest you are?"

Andrew ignored the woman's outstretched hand, and she dropped it back to her side.

"I'm here to see…" he started, then cleared his throat. "Robert MacAllister."

"Uncle Robert?" she said, smiling. "Why don't I take you to his table. I could be wrong, but I believe you're the last guest to arrive. I'm just standing here looking ridiculous."

No, she was looking beautiful, Andrew thought. Absolutely lovely. Her short, curly, black hair framed a face of exquisite features including a smile that made her dark eyes sparkle.

And her lips. They gave a whole new meaning to the word *kissable*.

Damn it, Malone. Did you catch the lady's name? *MacAllister*. Kara *MacAllister*.

"Where's Robert MacAllister?" he said gruffly.

Kara frowned. "You don't exactly seem in the party mood, Mr.… I don't believe you mentioned your name."

"It's Malone. Andrew Malone."

"Well, Mr. Malone, please allow me to welcome you to the final event of the weeklong MacAllister reunion."

Andrew nodded absently.

"Would you follow me please, Mr. Malone?" Kara said with a sweep of one arm.

Andrew nodded, then fell in step behind Kara as she made her way through the maze of tables. His glance slid down Kara's back, and a jolt of heat slammed through him as he noticed the sway of her hips and the way the soft material of her dress clung enticingly to her feminine curves.

Damn it, Malone. She's a MacAllister.

Kara stopped, causing Andrew to nearly bump into her. She looked up at him and smiled. "You're in luck," she said. "Uncle Robert and Aunt Margaret are heading back to their table from the buffet. There's Uncle Robert coming our way. See?"

Andrew's heart thundered and a trickle of sweat ran down his chest.

Robert MacAllister. It was hard to believe the man was only a few feet away and coming closer every second.

"Uncle Robert?" she said, before Robert had a chance to take his place at the table. "I've brought one of your guests so you can say hello."

Robert frowned as he looked at Andrew. "*My* guest? I'm sorry, but Kara must have misunderstood you. I don't believe you and I have met."

"We haven't," Andrew said, his gaze riveted on Robert.

"But you told me that…" Kara started, obviously confused.

"I said I was here to see Robert MacAllister," Andrew said, not looking at Kara. "I didn't say that he'd invited me."

"What do you want?" Kara said.

"Kara," Robert said, "I'm sure there's a reasonable explanation for why Mr—"

"Malone. Andrew Malone," Andrew said.

"Why Mr. Malone has come here," Robert said. "Would you care to clue us in, young man?"

"I'm here," Andrew said, a muscle jumping along his jaw, "because it's time. In fact, it's long overdue. The name Malone doesn't mean anything to you?''

"No, it doesn't," Robert said thoughtfully. "Should it?"

"I suppose not," Andrew said, a rough tone to his voice. "It didn't mean anything then, so why should it now?"

"Look, I'm afraid I'm going to have to ask you to leave," Robert said. "I have no idea why you're here, but this is a private party and—"

"For family only," Andrew said. "I know. That's why I'm here. You forgot to send me my invitation. Does the name *Sally* Malone conjure up any memories, Robert? A summer a long time ago? An innocent young girl who fell in love with you? Hey, come on, Robert, surely you remember Sally."

The color drained from Robert's face as he stared at Andrew. "Sally Malone," Robert said, hardly above a whisper. "I'd forgotten all about her."

"You forgot her the minute she was out of your sight," Andrew said with a sharp bark of laughter. "But she never forgot you, Robert. Oh, she never forgot you."

"Robert, what is going on?" Margaret MacAllister said from her place at the table. "Who is Sally Malone?"

"My mother," Andrew said, taking a step closer to Robert. "My mother who died when I was fifteen years old. My mother who had *your* baby after you abandoned her that summer, MacAllister. Let me introduce myself again. I'm Andrew Malone. *Your son.*"

"What?" Kara said.

"Robert?" Margaret said, a frantic edge to her voice. "What is he saying? What does this mean?"

"My God," Robert said, his eyes holding Andrew's. "You're... Oh— Oh, pain...I..."

Robert pressed both fists to his chest and collapsed to the floor, knocking over his chair.

It was bedlam. Margaret screamed Robert's name and jumped to her feet as people at other tables rose and turned in the direction of the commotion. Everyone seemed to be talking at once as Margaret dropped to her knees beside her husband.

"Get out of my way," Kara said, pushing past Andrew. "Move."

Andrew took a step backward as people began to hurry to where Robert lay on the floor, his eyes closed. Kara knelt beside her uncle, pulled his tie down and undid the top two buttons of his shirt. She looked up and quickly scanned the crowd.

"Give him air," she yelled. "Ryan, I need help here with CPR. Forrest, call 9-1-1. Hurry up. We need an ambulance, paramedics. Tell them to contact Mercy Hospital where I'm on staff and tell those on duty in the emergency room to stand by for our arrival. I think Uncle Robert has had a heart attack!"

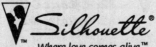

MONTANA MAVERICKS

Montana Mavericks: Wed in Whitehorn
Stories that capture living and loving beneath the
Big Sky, where legends live on and love lasts forever!

Silhouette® brings you a BRAND-NEW program that includes
12 incredible stories that will take you to Whitehorn,
Montana, where love and mystery are always in the air!

Watch for the first book in June 2000 at
your favorite retail outlet.

LONE STALLION'S LADY
by **Lisa Jackson**

Use this coupon on any Montana Mavericks title
and receive $1 off.

Visit Silhouette at www.eHarlequin.com   MM100US

MONTANA MAVERICKS

Montana Mavericks: Wed in Whitehorn
Stories that capture living and loving beneath the
Big Sky, where legends live on and love lasts forever!

Silhouette® brings you a BRAND-NEW program that includes
12 incredible stories that will take you to Whitehorn,
Montana, where love and mystery are always in the air!

Watch for the first book in June 2000 at
your favorite retail outlet.

LONE STALLION'S LADY
by **Lisa Jackson**

Use this coupon on any Montana Mavericks title
and receive $1 off.

Silhouette®

SPECIAL EDITION™®

COMING NEXT MONTH